PLAYING FAVORITES

Also by Trevor Kew
in the Lorimer Sports Stories series:

Breakaway
Sidelined
Trading Goals

PLAYING FAVORITES

Trevor Kew

James Lorimer & Company Ltd., Publishers
Toronto

James Lorimer & Company Ltd., Publishers acknowledges the support of
the Ontario Arts Council. We acknowledge the financial support of the
Government of Canada through the Canada Book Fund for our publishing
activities. We acknowledge the support of the Canada Council for the Arts
which last year invested $24.3 million in writing and publishing throughout
Canada. We acknowledge the Government of Ontario through the Ontario
Media Development Corporation's Ontario Book Initiative.

Cover Image: Shutterstock

Library and Archives Canada Cataloguing in Publication

Kew, Trevor
        Playing favourites / Trevor Kew.

(Sports stories)
Issued also in an electronic format.
ISBN 978-1-4594-0257-7 (bound).--ISBN 978-1-4594-0256-0 (pbk.)

        I. Title. II. Series: Sports stories (Toronto, Ont.)

PS8621.E95P53 2012   jC813'.6   C2012-903690-0

James Lorimer & Company Ltd.,   Distributed in the United States by:
Publishers   Orca Book Publishers
317 Adelaide Street West, Suite 1002 P.O. Box 468
Toronto, ON, Canada   Custer, WA USA
M5V 1P9   98240-0468
www.lorimer.ca

Printed and bound in Canada.
Manufactured by Friesens Corporation in Altona, Manitoba, Canada in
August 2012.
Job #77080

For Mr. Gillingham — thank you for all those Soccer Saturdays

CONTENTS

1 FOUL PLAY

"Mido! Over here!"

Gavin dug his cleats into the soft ground and sprinted toward the goal. "Over here!" he yelled again.

On the left side of the field, Gavin's friend Mido had the ball at his feet. He stepped past a big defender and crossed the ball into the danger area. Gavin leaped as high as he could, but the cross just cleared his head.

He turned and saw the ball in the opposing goalkeeper's hands.

"Good try, Gav!" shouted Mido.

The keeper kicked long. A forward received the ball on his thigh, nudged it to his right, then smashed a shot toward the bottom left corner. At the last moment, a pair of long arms stretched out and snagged the ball out of mid-air.

"Great save, Critter!"

Gavin watched their goalkeeper scramble to his feet. Critter was unbelievable. Even with his long, lanky limbs he was quick, alert, and could catch almost anything. Mido, the smallest player on the team, had once said the guy was half-octopus and half-giraffe. That's why everyone called him Critter.

Critter's long throw soared into the opposition's half of the field. Pushing past a defender, Gavin stretched to get to the ball first. He spun around, faked left, then went right. Two defenders lunged and missed. The goalkeeper moved out to cut down the angle.

"Gavin!" called a voice to his left. He glanced sideways and saw Mido.

Ignoring his friend, he sent a shot curling around the keeper. It bounced in off the far post.

"Nice shot," said Mido.

Gavin felt a little guilty, high-fiving his friend. He knew he could have passed instead of scoring himself. But Mido had a special talent for missing empty nets, and Gavin wanted to win.

The referee blew his whistle three times. Players from both teams jogged over to the side of the field.

It was halftime at their final match of the summer in the City Seven-a-Side League. Gavin's team, the Kingsgate Lions, was made up of ten best friends from his middle school soccer team.

Nine best friends, Gavin corrected himself, catching a glimpse of Craig O'Connor on the sidelines. Craig was standing with some of the other substitutes, laughing as he juggled a soccer ball. Gavin noticed that he was wearing a new pair of boots, his third pair of the summer. These ones were orange and white.

Craig never bothered warming up. He never even stretched. He acted like he was too gifted to bother with that kind of stuff.

Hard to pull a muscle when you're that lazy, thought Gavin.

"Good hustle, Lions!"

Gavin looked up and saw Mr. O'Connor walking onto the field. One again, he seemed to have forgotten the water bottles. All around, players' shirts were drenched with sweat under the hot August sun.

"Good game, guys," said Mr. O'Connor, clapping his hands together. "You really attacked their end zone and crashed their defence."

Gavin heard Mido snort behind him. Mr. O'Connor was always bragging about his time as a football quarterback at university. He seemed to think it made him an authority on every sport, including soccer. It didn't.

But Mr. O'Connor had been the only parent willing to coach their summer team. There had been one condition: His son Craig had to be on the team.

"Gonna shake things up this half, fellas," said Mr. O'Connor. "Keep 'em guessing, you know? We'll throw Noel in at left defenceman —"

Another snort from Mido.

"— and Craig in for Mido up forward in . . . What's that position called again? Streaker?"

Striker. Someone groaned.

"But ... but ... Craig always plays right back," Mido burst out. "And I already subbed off once in the first half!"

Mr. O'Connor cleared his throat. "Yeah, but we need to win this game, Mido. And I think we need someone out there who can really dipsy-doodle around their defencemen."

Gavin knew he should speak up and support his friend against the coach. But somehow the words wouldn't come.

Behind them, the referee whistled for the teams to return to the field.

Mido shook his head in disbelief. "Defencemen," he muttered under his breath. "End zone. Shake things up. Dipsy-doodle."

The Lions were ahead in the match 3–0, but their work wasn't finished yet. To win the summer league championship, they needed to score at least six goals.

Gavin had scored all three goals in the first half. He was sure he could get three more.

Lining up in the centre circle, he glanced over at Craig standing there lazily in his orange-and-white boots. *That guy cares more about the way he looks than about winning the match*, he decided.

He is *more skilful than Mido though*, Gavin thought, feeling guilty once more.

The whistle sounded. Gavin tapped the ball to his teammate.

"Watch this," Craig said.

Gavin watched as Craig slipped the ball past one opponent. He did a fancy step-over fake. Then another. And another. His orange boots flashed as he flipped the ball up into the air and caught it on his foot.

"Hey, cross it!" shouted Gavin, sprinting forward.

Craig ignored him and dribbled past one defender, then another. He tried a shot from a wide angle, which soared high over the net.

Gavin clenched his fists in frustration. "Why didn't you pass?"

"Shut up," Craig sneered. "You just wish you had my skills."

Maybe if I wanted to be in the circus, thought Gavin. *But this is a soccer game. I want to win.*

The goal kick from the opposing goalkeeper was a bad one. Gavin intercepted it easily and raced toward the goal. He slipped the ball past the keeper and into the back of the net.

4–0!

A few minutes later, he tackled a defender cleanly, taking the ball. This time, as the goalkeeper charged, Gavin saw Craig to his right. He ignored him and slotted the ball into the goal himself.

As Gavin jogged back, he could hear Craig behind him, swearing loudly.

Mido cheered from the sidelines. "Come on, guys — one more goal!"

"Coach!" shouted Critter from the goal. "Put Mido back on. It's his turn!"

Mr. O'Connor waved him away. "Not now."

Gavin was sure Mido was going to lose it on the coach, but he didn't. He just kept clapping his hands, encouraging his teammates to score one more.

How can he stand it? Gavin wondered. *If Coach O'Connor treated me like that, I'd go home.*

When they kicked off again, Craig nicked the ball right off Gavin's boot. He then did more step-overs than Gavin had thought possible for a single human soccer player. Two defenders were fooled but a third tackled the ball away.

Gavin lunged in, winning the ball back. He swerved past a diving defender. He tried to shoot, but someone barged into his shoulder, knocking him to the turf.

He looked up and saw Craig standing over him. Unbelievable! He'd been fouled by his own teammate.

Craig's shot soared over the net again.

Minutes later, at the other end of the field, Critter caught a high cross. He kicked the ball forward. Gavin reached it first. He slipped the ball through a defender's legs, then swung his right foot to shoot.

Whoosh! Nothing but air.

He spun around in horror, just in time to see Craig slice a shot wide of the far post.

"What's wrong with you?" Gavin hollered. "What do you think you're doing?"

Craig glared back at him.

The teams battled in midfield for a moment until the ball popped loose, right to Gavin. He took a long shot before Craig could get near him. The goalkeeper tipped it over the bar for a corner kick.

"Gavin!" shouted Mido from the sidelines. "Two minutes left. Let's get everyone up there! You too, Critter. Everyone!"

The tall goalkeeper started running forward.

This was it. Last chance. Do or die. Time to risk it all.

But then Gavin saw Mr. O'Connor, red-faced, waving Critter back. "Critter, what are you doing? You're the goaltender. Get back in the goal!"

Critter slowed, then stopped at the halfway line. He looked right at Gavin, obviously unsure what to do.

Gavin glanced at Mr. O'Connor, then at Mido, then back at their empty goal. He shrugged at his lanky friend. Critter hesitated, but then turned and began to jog back.

Mido threw up his hands in disbelief.

The corner kick flew into the area, curling away from the goalkeeper's reaching hands. It was perfectly lined up for Gavin. He leaped into the air, aiming his forehead at the ball.

There was a hard shove against his back, right between the shoulder blades. His face thudded into the grass. He heard the ball smack someone else's forehead.

Rolling over, he saw the ball loop high and wide of the net.

Somewhere in the distance, the referee's whistle sounded three times, ending the match.

5–0. One goal short of the championship.

Gavin climbed to his feet. He saw Craig, with his mean pock-marked face, and glared back at him.

"Don't blame me, ball hog," snapped Craig. "I had that header lined up. You were in my way."

Gavin said fiercely, "I'll get you for this."

"Whatever," laughed Craig. "Who cares about this stupid summer league? After next week, I'll be on the best soccer team in the city. You and Critter and Mido will all be stuck at Vandyke."

2 SOCCER SATURDAY

When Gavin awoke the next morning, his bedroom was filled with the bright sunshine of late summer. He rolled over and squinted. The curtains had been left open from the night before.

He groaned and pulled the covers over his head. Three more days before the start of high school. Just three more days.

Which meant it was Saturday.

Soccer Saturday!

Gavin pushed himself up and leaped out of bed. Tugging on a pair of old sweatpants, he rushed out of his bedroom.

As he hurried down the stairs, he heard a shout.

"Come on! What are you doing? There's no time! Go for it!"

As he walked into the living room, Gavin caught sight of Mido. His friend was perched on the edge of the couch, hands held out toward the television. He was wearing his red Liverpool jersey. Critter lounged lazily against some pillows at the other end of the couch.

Beside them sat Gavin's grandfather, settled into his favourite old brown chair. A newspaper was folded on his lap, and a steaming cup of tea rested on a little round table next to him.

"Morning, Granddad," said Gavin. "Mom and Dad not up yet?"

"Morning, sleepyhead," replied Granddad. "You just missed them. They went out for a walk down by the lake."

The old man pointed at the television. "You've slept through a cracking game. Isn't that right, Middle?"

Gavin caught Critter grinning. Granddad was from England, where Gavin's mom had grown up. Critter couldn't get enough of Granddad's accent and strange expressions. No matter how many times Gavin told the old man that Mido's name was pronounced *Mee-do*, it always came out sounding something like *middle* or *midd-o*.

"We've been so unlucky, Gav," said Mido, his eyes fixed on the screen. "Manchester United scored on one lucky chance. We've hit the post twice. It's not fair."

Granddad picked up his tea cup and looked at Mido over the brim. "Yeah, I reckon you're right. It's not fair. Too many coats of paint on those posts."

Critter laughed. "Nice, Mr. Gillingham. I've never heard that one before."

Gavin shook his head. "Me neither. Granddad's

always got a new one up his sleeve."

Mido collapsed onto the floor dramatically. "Why don't you learn how to coach?" he complained.

"What's the problem, Meeds?" asked Gavin, sitting down between his friends.

Mido pointed at the screen. "This new Liverpool manager never takes a risk. There's two minutes left. He needs to push all his players forward and go for it!" He looked sideways at Gavin. "Sort of like us yesterday — not bringing up Critter."

Gavin remembered and felt a sudden knot in his stomach. His friend was probably right about yesterday's game. But the way Mido made it seem like his fault annoyed him.

Critter came to the rescue. "I would've just fallen on my face anyway. Or caught the ball with my hands and had a free kick called against me."

Everyone laughed at that.

"Say, Mr. G," Critter went on, "what's that English team you cheer for again? The one nobody's heard of?"

"Ipswich Town," replied Granddad proudly, "a proper football team." He pointed at the screen. "Not like these overpaid fools with their silly haircuts and Ferraris and orange football boots."

Liverpool's striker blasted an easy tap-in over the bar. Mido put his head in his hands.

"See?" said Granddad, shaking his head. "I could've done that. And he makes ten million pounds a year for it. And look — what'd I tell ya? Orange boots."

The final whistle sounded onscreen, ending the match. Mido collapsed onto the floor again.

Granddad rose slowly from the armchair. "Are you lot hungry?"

"Yes, please!" exclaimed Mido and Critter at the same time.

"Gavin?"

"Yes, thanks, Granddad."

The old man nodded, then turned and left the room.

On the television, two commentators at a studio table were discussing the Liverpool–Manchester United match. Gavin grabbed the remote control and turned the volume down.

"What's up, Gav?" said Mido. "You seem a bit quiet this morning."

Craig's words after the game rattled through Gavin's brain for the hundredth time. *I'll be on the best soccer team in the city. You and Critter and Mido will all be stuck at Vandyke.*

He shrugged. "I don't know. I guess just . . . yesterday and losing the game . . . and Craig . . ."

Critter jumped in. "Ah Gav, who cares about that idiot?"

"I care!" Mido exclaimed. "He and his dad lost us the summer championship."

"It's not just that," said Gavin. "It's what he said about high school. He's right. I mean, he's going to St.

Mike's and we're going to stupid old Vandyke."

"Who wants to go to St. Mike's, anyway?" said Critter. "Private school. Bunch of snotty rich kids."

"Fair enough," said Gavin. "But they win the city soccer championship every year. And Vandyke, well . . ."

They all fell silent for a moment. They'd had the same conversation over and over all summer. After three straight years of winning the city championships at Kingsgate Middle School, Gavin, Critter, and Mido were heading to a high school famous for just one thing: football. Not the football with keepers and red cards and goalkeeping gloves. The North American version, with all its helmets and first downs and touchdown dances.

"If only this was England," said Gavin, "where football means soccer, instead of that other stupid meathead sport."

"American football's so dumb," said Mido. "They think they're so tough, but look at all that padding they wear."

Granddad came back into the living room. "Is the footie back on yet, chaps?"

"Chaps," chuckled Critter. "Footie."

"Are you mocking the Queen's English, young man?" said Granddad.

"No, of course not, sir," replied Critter.

"Well, hurry up, then. Grab yourself a plate, lads," said the old man.

They followed him into the kitchen.

"That smells amazing!" exclaimed Critter.

Three full English breakfasts — eggs, sausages, bacon, beans, toast, and grilled tomoates — were lined up on the kitchen counter.

Critter finished his bacon before he'd even left the kitchen.

"Thanks, Mr. G.," he mumbled through a mouthful of beans.

"Yeah, thanks. It's delicious!" exclaimed Mido.

It wasn't until the four of them had settled back in the living room to watch the second match that Gavin noticed what Granddad was eating. The old man was munching away on a bowl full of granola and fruit.

"Cereal, Granddad?" asked Gavin, confused.

"Yeah," grumbled Granddad, stirring his breakfast half-heartedly with a spoon. "Your mother says I need to watch my weight. Don't know why. Not like I'll be going out dancing any time soon."

Critter stopped eating. "Oh, I don't know, Mr. G. —"

"Quiet, you!" said Granddad with a grin.

They sat and watched the rest of the match. Aston Villa ended up beating Chelsea 3–0.

When the match had finished, Granddad gathered up their plates and took them away to the kitchen. When he returned, he sat down and leaned back in his chair.

"Did I ever tell you chaps about the football team I started with my mates back in Ipswich?" he asked.

"Don't think so," said Mido.

"Nope," said Critter.

Gavin shook his head.

Granddad leaned forward. "It was when I was seventeen," he said. "A bunch of us had already left school, and were working down at the brickworks. We all loved football. There was just one problem. We didn't have Saturdays off, and that was when the league played its matches."

"What'd you do?" asked Mido.

"Well, we all just stood around grumbling about it for days and days until a little lad — Sweeney, his name was — got fed up. He marched right up to our big foreman and asked for Saturday afternoons off so that we could play football."

"What'd he say?" asked Critter.

"Nothing. The foreman bopped him on the nose," replied Granddad. "But little Sweeney kept going up and asking every day and eventually the foreman agreed. But only if he could play too, in central midfield."

"Was he any good?" asked Gavin.

"Bloody awful," said Granddad, shaking his head, "but boy, did we ever have fun on that team. I'd give anything to play one more game with those lads.

"Anyway," he said, tapping his finger on the armrest of his chair, "guess I'd best be off for a shave and a bath." He turned toward Critter and Mido. "See you two next weekend for Soccer Saturday?"

"You bet!" said Critter. "You know us *chaps*. We never miss the *footie*!"

3 A SCHOOL WITHOUT SOCCER

Gavin, Critter, and Mido stood together, staring at the big red-brick building across the road.

It was strange, Gavin thought. During middle school, they'd walked past Vandyke every day. But today, the walls of the high school seemed bigger than they ever had before.

"I can't believe we're in high school," said Critter.

They crossed the road and stepped onto the school field. Gavin looked down at the football yard markings chalked across the grass in white. There were large football uprights at both ends of the field.

In the distance, Gavin spotted two soccer nets pushed into a corner, up against the fence.

The field was full of students. Right away, Gavin noticed a large group of guys standing next to the school's main entrance. They were all wearing the same black jackets with orange-gold writing on the sleeves: Vandyke Tigers. A bunch of pretty girls hovered around them. As Mido walked past the group, he turned and looked back at Gavin and Critter.

"Did you see those guys?" he said as they entered the main school building. "Some of them were the size of my dad's car."

"Whatever," said Gavin once they were inside. "They're football players. I bet they'd run out of gas after five minutes on a soccer field."

But he was pretty sure he wouldn't say that to their faces.

"Forget about the guys," said Critter. "Did you see those girls?"

Inside the school, students were everywhere: chatting, laughing, leaning against lockers. None of them paid any attention to Gavin and his two best friends as they walked past.

The bell rang.

"I think my homeroom is this way," said Mido, pointing behind them. "Sucks that I'm not with you guys." He headed off in the opposite direction.

"Where are we supposed to go, Gav?" asked Critter.

Gavin opened a pocket in his backpack and pulled out a piece of paper. "Room 105."

"Oh," said Critter, gesturing with one of his gangly arms. "That's right over there."

When they entered the classroom, most of the students were already sitting down. Gavin and Critter took two seats near the back.

A chubby guy with red hair sat down next to Gavin.

"Hey man, what's up?" he said.

"Not much," Gavin replied. He turned toward Critter and raised his eyebrows.

Their teacher entered the room. He was a tall man with massive arms and shoulders. His head was shaved bald and there was a long curved scar running down the left side of his face. He wore a white-collared T-shirt with VANDYKE TIGERS FOOTBALL on the front and a pair of blue gym shorts.

He strode to the head of the class. "Welcome to the big leagues," he said.

Gavin saw a few students exchange worried looks. He glanced at Critter. Critter usually never paid attention to teachers. But right now his eyes were fixed on the front of the room.

"Look, I'm going to level with you. You're not in middle school anymore," said the teacher. "This is the real world. We are not here to baby you."

Silence again. More worried looks between students.

"My name is Mr. Sonderhoff," he said. "But everyone around here calls me Coach."

Coach went through the attendance roster, then started into school rules. It was all the usual stuff. Don't chew gum. Don't be late for classes. Don't forget to do your homework.

Gavin's mind began to wander. He thought about his middle school soccer team. He remembered how great it had felt to hold that championship trophy three years in a row. What would it be like this year to play for a team that never won?

He imagined a giant scoreboard: St. Mike's 10, Vandyke 0. He pictured Craig's sneering face.

"Hey, wake up, buddy," said the chubby red-haired student. He handed Gavin a piece of paper.

"What's this?" Gavin whispered.

The red-haired guy leaned over. "Coach says it's a sign-up sheet for activities this semester." He paused, then asked, "You guys trying out for football?"

"Football?" Gavin laughed. "Why would we want to do that?"

"Well, what sport do you play, then?"

"Soccer," said Gavin.

"Oh yeah," replied the redhead. "I played that back in middle school too."

Gavin shot a surprised look at Critter. *How on earth had this chunky guy played on a soccer team?*

But Critter didn't notice. He was staring hard at the form on his desk. "Gav, soccer's not listed here."

Gavin snatched up his own piece of paper.

Badminton, football, cheerleading, jazz band, chess club . . . No soccer.

"Maybe it's a mistake," said Critter.

The bell rang and students began to file out of the classroom. On their way, they handed their forms to Mr. Sonderhoff.

"Excuse me, Coach," said Gavin, holding out his

own form. "There's no soccer on here. Is it a mistake?"

Mr. Sonderhoff shook his head. "Unfortunately, it's no mistake. Our soccer coach moved to Toronto last year. We haven't been able to find a replacement."

"But . . ." began Gavin, his voice wavering.

"Sorry, guys," shrugged their teacher. He pointed to their red-haired classmate. "Say — why don't you two join Derek and try out for football?"

***

In the two classes between homeroom and lunch, Gavin sat staring at the walls. He barely heard a word that his French teacher or his math teacher said. Just that morning, he'd come to school worried about playing for the worst team in the city.

Only it wasn't the worst team anymore. It was no team at all.

After math class, Gavin and Critter walked to the cafeteria in silence. They filled their trays with spaghetti and salad, then found Mido. He was sitting alone, his food already half-eaten.

"Boy, am I happy to see you guys," he said. "Advanced Math is full of nerds! They spent the whole class bragging about their grades in middle school."

Neither Gavin nor Critter said anything in reply.

"What's with you guys?" asked Mido.

"This school sucks," Gavin mumbled through a

mouthful of spaghetti. The food sucked, too. It was lukewarm and almost tasteless.

"Tell me about it," Mido agreed. "I just know my parents are gonna make me join the debate club and the green club and all the other usual —"

"Mido," Gavin interrupted. "There's no soccer team."

"*What?*" Mido knocked over his bottle of orange juice. Luckily, he'd almost finished, so only a little spilled. He righted the bottle and looked at Gavin, then Critter. "Tell me this isn't true. You guys are kidding, right?"

Critter shook his head. "The coach of the football team told us."

"But . . . but . . . we've got to do something about this!" exclaimed Mido. "We can't just not have a team."

"You're right," said Gavin. "But what can we do?" He looked around the cafeteria. "I knew something like this was going to happen here. I just knew it."

"This school sucks," said Mido.

Gavin took one more mouthful of the bland spaghetti, then pushed the plate aside. The three friends sat staring down at the table, the noise of students all around them.

Then Critter sat up straight. "I've got it!" He turned toward Gavin. "You remember what your grandfather said — about the team he and his friends started? Why don't we do that?"

It was like someone had flipped the light switch on in a dark room.

"You know what?" said Gavin, nodding. "That just might work."

"So how do we do it?" asked Mido.

"Well," replied Critter. "The guy in charge of sports at this school seems to be Coach Sonderhoff, so I guess we need to talk to him. Why don't you talk to him, Gav?"

"Me?" cried Gavin. "What about you?"

Critter shook his head. "I'd say something stupid and mess it up."

Mido spoke up. "Guys, why don't you let *me* handle it?"

Gavin stopped and thought for a moment. After speaking to Coach Sonderhoff that morning, he wasn't exactly eager for another conversation. But at least the teacher already knew him. He'd have no idea who Mido was.

"Thanks," Gavin told his friend. "But since he's our homeroom teacher, I guess I'm the best one to talk to him. Later today, maybe."

"How about now?" said Critter. "He's right over there."

Gavin turned around. Coach was standing on the other side of the cafeteria, leaning against a wall. He was talking to three older students wearing Tigers jackets. He looked angry.

Gavin stood up. He took a deep breath.

Walking across the cafeteria, he recalled his

grandfather's story. What was the guy's name, the one who'd asked for Saturdays off to play soccer? Smitty? Stanley? Whatever it was, the guy who'd asked had been bopped on the nose. Getting bopped on the nose — it sounded funny, almost friendly. Gavin was pretty sure it wasn't.

Teachers can't hit students, he told himself. It didn't make him feel any better. He was close enough now to see that Coach Sonderhoff was really annoyed. So annoyed that a large blue vein was throbbing in his forehead.

As Gavin approached, the football players walked away, their shoulders slumped.

Coach glared after them. "Lazy, good-for-nothing . . ." He turned toward Gavin. "What do you want?"

Gavin opened his mouth. The words didn't come.

The coach raised an eyebrow. "Well? What is it?"

"I . . ." began Gavin. He swallowed. "I know you said there is no soccer team this year, Coach. And I respect that."

I respect that? Gavin felt like kicking himself.

"Glad to hear it," said Coach. He didn't sound very interested.

Gavin tried again. "It's just that . . . well, some of the guys and I were talking and, well, we really want a soccer team. You said the coach left. But isn't there a teacher who could maybe just stand there and supervise us?"

"Look, I'm sorry," said Coach Sonderhoff, shaking his head. "I asked every teacher in the school. Everyone's too busy."

"It's just . . . it's just . . ." Gavin looked away from Coach's forbidding scowl. "Ah, never mind."

He turned and began to walk away.

I should have let Mido do this, Gavin thought regretfully. *He would have known what to say.*

"What's your name again, kid?"

Gavin turned around. He was shocked to see a smile on Coach Sonderhoff's face. Well, not a smile, exactly. Something sort of like a smile.

"Gavin," he said. "Gavin Harrison."

"Look, Gavin," said Coach. "I admire your guts, coming up to talk to me on your first day. Maybe we can work something out. What if I give you the far end of the field during our football practices? It's a scruffy piece of ground, but it's better than nothing."

I'd play in the parking lot if that's all there was, thought Gavin. "Yeah!" he blurted out. "I mean, wow. Thanks so much!"

"You're welcome," said the big man.

He looked at Gavin, then raised an eyebrow. "So, you've got a team. Maybe I can supervise, but who's the coach?"

4 WHO'S THE COACH?

"Morning, Gav."

Gavin rubbed his eyes, then yawned. His mother was sitting on the living-room couch, a cup of coffee next to her on the side table. She was reading a book.

"Morning, Mom." Gavin flopped down onto a chair. He glanced over at the book in her hands. *Medieval Russian History*. He shook his head. Sometimes he wondered if his mother really came from this planet.

"Where's Granddad?" he asked, snatching up the remote control and switching on the television.

"Your father drove him to the drugstore to get his prescriptions filled," she replied. She put down her book. "Guess Critter and Mido will be here soon, eh? How about I make you all some breakfast? Muesli and yogurt?"

Gavin was about to explain that Soccer Saturday wouldn't be the same without a full English breakfast, but something stopped him. Mom was just being nice, after all. And her breakfasts weren't that bad. With a bit of fruit and yogurt on top, he could almost forget that muesli tasted like sawdust.

On television, two teams were warming up: Wolverhampton and Chelsea. Long ago, when he was very little and Granddad had just moved to Canada, Gavin had chosen Wolves to be his team. He'd wanted to support Chelsea, because they'd been champions that year, but Granddad had mocked him for being a "glory supporter." And so Gavin had chosen Wolves, because he'd liked their orange jerseys.

It wasn't always easy. At the moment, Wolves had lost ten of their last eleven matches. Their fans were angry. Their coach had been fired.

A close-up of the new coach appeared onscreen. He was a tall man with a long pointy nose. He was wearing a black suit jacket and sporting an orange Wolves tie. His eyes were darting back and forth rapidly as he scanned the field.

Gavin thought he looked nervous.

Who's the coach? Coach Sonderhoff's words echoed through Gavin's head for the thousandth time that week.

Do we really need one? Gavin wondered. *Maybe things would be better without a coach.* He thought about the summer league and Mr. O'Connor, Craig's father. *Maybe coaches just mess everything up.*

He heard the front door open and close. A moment later, Granddad walked in.

He chuckled as he removed his peaked cap and un-buttoned his thick coat. "All right, mate? Wolves play-ing today? Ready for a right thumping from Chelsea?"

Gavin's father burst into the room, Mido and Critter right behind him. "Look who we dragged in from the street!" he exclaimed.

"Hey guys," Gavin said.

His father pointed at the television. "Ooh, big *foot-ball* game today, I see. Is Brazil playing?"

Gavin saw Granddad turn away to hide his smile.

"Dad," he groaned, "it's the English Premier League, not the World Cup. Countries aren't playing each other. It's more like the Canucks playing the Flames."

Gavin's father understood hockey better than soc-cer. But only a little. Neither of his parents cared much about sports. They only pretended to, for his sake. At least his mother didn't try as hard as his father.

"Got your Wolves jersey on, eh, Gav?" said Critter, parking himself on the couch.

Mido settled on the couch too, then scoffed, "Wolves — who's ever heard of them?"

"They're a team for real soccer fans, not glory sup-porters," said Gavin. He pointed at the Wolves crest on his shirt. "3-0 for us, just you watch."

"Hey, by the way, what do *our* team jerseys look like this year, Gav?" asked Mido.

Gavin was caught off guard. "I . . . I'm not sure," he said. "I haven't seen them yet."

Who's the Coach?

Mido turned back to the television. "Never mind. I was just wondering."

All week, Mido had been asking Gavin questions about things like uniforms and practice drills and team strategy. It worried Gavin, because he didn't have any answers.

"Did you find out when our first practice is?" Mido asked.

"I . . . I'm still not sure," said Gavin. "Coach Sonderhoff said he'd let me know on Monday. He's got to finish cutting the football team first."

"Football?" said Gavin's grandfather scornfully. "You mean that game with the big leather egg? Should be called hand-egg, if you ask me."

Critter laughed.

On the TV screen, the blond Chelsea striker dribbled around the Wolves keeper and scored into the open goal.

Gavin groaned.

"Great goal, eh?" said Mido.

"Only 1–0, Gav," said Critter. "Still lots of time left."

Granddad leaned forward in his old brown chair. "So, lads," he said, "I hear you have yourselves a team at school."

Gavin was about to reply, but Mido beat him to it. "Yeah, Critter got the idea from your story about England, Mr. G."

"Wonderful, Midd-o!" declared Granddad. "Gavin,

you've been talking about the team all week, but you never told me my boring old story was behind it!"

Chelsea scored again. Gavin punched a seat cushion. "Damn!"

"What's that sound?" said Mido, holding a hand to his ear. "Oh — it's the thud of Wolves hitting the bottom of the league table!"

Critter and Granddad laughed.

"Good one, Middle," said Granddad. "Well played."

Gavin laughed a little. He was annoyed that his team was losing. But last week Mido had been the one to suffer when his team, Liverpool, had lost to Manchester United.

"Not looking too good, Gav," said Critter, pointing at the screen. Wolves' new coach was pacing and shouting at his players. "Tough start for the new coach."

Gavin's mother entered the room, carrying bowls of fruit and muesli.

"Breakfast, fellas," she announced.

Mido looked down at the food. "Uh, thanks, Mrs. Harrison."

Critter didn't seem too excited either. "Yeah . . . thank you very much, Mrs. H."

Gavin saw his grandfather moving a spoon gingerly through the cereal. "The fruit on top looks nice enough," he whispered in the boys' direction once Gavin's mom had left the room. "The rest looks like something you feed to cows."

Who's the Coach?

Gavin scooped up a spoonful of muesli, banana, and yogurt. It actually tasted pretty good. But it was no match for Granddad's English breakfasts.

He saw Granddad finish the fruit on top of his cereal, then slide the bowl as far away as possible.

"Hey, Mr. G," said Mido. "What was your coach like? You know, back when you guys started that team?"

Granddad scratched his forehead. "Hmm, let me think. Well, our old gaffer was pretty strict."

"Gaffer?" asked Mido.

"Our manager," explained Granddad. "He sure was a tough old bloke. He'd been a sergeant major in the Second World War, I think. Made us run so much, some of the lads used to joke he was training us for the bloody Olympics! Lads used to throw up sometimes, cursing his name under their breath."

"Why didn't someone complain?" exclaimed Gavin. He couldn't imagine playing for a coach like that. Soccer wasn't about running laps until you puked. It was about clever tricks and scorching goals and stellar saves. It was about having fun. Most of all, it was about winning.

Granddad shook his head. "We were all terrified of him. If one of us stepped out of line, he'd make the whole team run until our legs felt like they were about to fall off. Tell you one thing, though — I'd never been so fit in my life."

"Hey, it's 3–0, Gav!" yelled Critter gleefully.

Gavin turned back to the television. The Chelsea players were celebrating. Again. Behind them, the Wolves goalkeeper lay in the grass, thumping the ground with his fist.

The game ended a few minutes later.

"Well, you were right about the score," said Mido, shoving Gavin's shoulder playfully.

The shove annoyed Gavin. But he told himself he wasn't being fair. Like Critter and Granddad, Mido was only joking around.

"Unlucky, mate," said Granddad, pushing himself up from his chair. "I'm off for a walk in the garden. See you lads next week." He pointed at the bowl of muesli. "I'll be sure to seize control of the kitchen first thing in the morning."

Before he left the room, he looked back at Gavin and his two friends. "If I were a few years younger, I'd be running out onto that football pitch with you. Nothing in the world could hold me back. Ah, well, I guess old age happens to us all.

"I can hardly wait for the dream team's first match," he added. "Keep me posted, will you?"

5 THE SPEECH

Critter, Mido, and Gavin had just reached the top of the school steps when they heard a man behind them shout. They all turned at once.

Coach Sonderhoff was coming across the playing field toward them.

"Morning, guys," he called out. "Gavin, you got a minute?"

Gavin gulped and looked at his friends.

"Want us to come along?" asked Mido.

Gavin thought, then shook his head. "Nah, it's okay. I'll catch you guys later."

He went back down the steps and jogged over to Coach Sonderhoff.

"Morning, Coach."

"Same to you," said the big man. He rapped his knuckles against one of the white metal football posts.

"Look, Gavin," he said at last, "I'll be honest with you. I love all sports. And so I want to support this soccer team. But I thought about it last night, and with

41

teaching and coaching football and everything else, I'm a very busy man."

Gavin could feel the palms of his hands beginning to sweat. Had Coach Sonderhoff changed his mind about supervising?

The coach continued. "That's why this soccer thing needs to be completely hassle-free for me. Training will be at the same time as our football practices, just like I told you last week. Down there." He pointed in the direction of the rough ground at the far end of the field. "And I'll sit in the stands during games. That's it."

Gavin breathed a sigh of relief. He nodded. "I understand, Coach."

Coach Sonderhoff handed Gavin a small key. "This opens the shed." He pointed to a small green building. "You'll be responsible for all the equipment — balls, bibs, cones — and uniforms too. And of course you'll need to run your own training sessions and deal with substitutions during games.

"Because, after all, you are the coach," he added, one eyebrow raised. "Aren't you?"

Gavin felt his face burn red at the word *coach*. "I guess I am."

"You might want to designate an assistant," said Coach Sonderhoff. "Coaching isn't as easy as it looks, you know. But I'll leave that up to you."

Immediately, Gavin thought of Mido. Mido would be a great assistant. In fact, Mido would be a great coach.

The Speech

Probably better than I would, thought Gavin. The idea worried him.

Coach Sonderhoff clapped his hands together. "I think that's everything," he said. "I'm making the last cuts from the football team tonight, so you can have your first practice tomorrow. Better get to class now."

As Gavin walked away, Coach Sonderhoff's question echoed through his mind. *You are the coach, aren't you?* For the first time, Gavin imagined the soccer team. He pictured them warming up for their first game. Brand-new jerseys. Brand-new boots. Perfect passes. Perfect shots. Perfect goals.

I'm the coach, he thought. *It's my team.*

That was the moment he decided not to make Mido his assistant.

"Hey, I almost forgot," Coach Sonderhoff called out after him. "There's an assembly in last period today. You can tell the whole school about the new team."

All Gavin's dreams of perfection and success disappeared in an instant. *A speech? In front of the whole school?*

"No problem," he lied, giving a thumbs-up. He walked away, thoughts racing, heart pounding.

Critter and Mido were waiting for him at the bottom of the steps.

"What'd he say, Gav?" asked Mido.

"Practice tomorrow," replied Gavin.

"Nice!" said Mido. He moved to high-five Gavin,

but stopped. "Hey, what's up? You okay?"

The school bell rang and students started to push past the three friends, heading for classes.

"I have to give a speech at the assembly today about the soccer team," Gavin confessed as they followed the other students through the door.

Critter started chuckling. "Sweet," he drawled. "I love seeing Gavin onstage."

"It's not funny," groaned Gavin.

"I know. You're right. Sorry, man."

They rounded a corner into the main hallway. Students were rushing in all directions.

"I've gotta go this way," said Mido, pointing up the stairs. "See you guys at the assembly?"

He started to walk away, then stopped and turned around. "You know, Gav, I could do it for you," he offered.

Gavin didn't reply.

"Just let me know," said Mido.

★★★

"Gavin, cut that out!" snapped Mr. Cowan from the front of the classroom.

Gavin jumped.

"What does he want me to cut out?" he whispered to Critter.

"You were tapping your pencil on the desk for like

five straight minutes," his friend replied, giving him a strange look.

Gavin had spent most of math class staring out the window, completely ignoring the worksheet on his desk. Now, he looked down at his notebook.

Question Seven. Not even half-finished.

He glanced up at the clock. Just five minutes to go. He put down his pencil. To hell with math. He had more important things on his mind. Such as how, in a few minutes, he'd be standing in front of hundreds and hundreds of high-school students.

He thought about the time he'd got up in front of his science class in Grade Seven to give a presentation on hurricanes. He'd researched the material, practised his speech with his father, written notes on little cards — everything. But when he got to the front of the class, he could barely speak. It was as if the words were frozen inside his brain.

And then, of course, there had been the horror of the school play in Grade Six. Mrs. Wilson had forced him to take a small part, just a single line. But when the time had come, Gavin had stuttered and stuttered until, unable to get the words out, he'd given up.

Some of the kids in middle school had teased him about it. Craig had been especially nasty. "G–G–Gavin . . . uhhh!" had been his favourite line for months after the play.

The bell sounded, ending the class.

"Okay, everyone," Mr. Cowan called out. "Down to the auditorium for assembly." He walked around checking their work. "Not your best effort today, I see," he murmured as he walked past Gavin's desk.

Walking down the stairs, Critter at his side, Gavin tried to tell himself it would all work out. It wasn't like he was running for prime minister. He only had to tell everyone that the soccer team's first practice was tomorrow after school.

Mido appeared next to them. "Hey guys, what's up?"

"Hey Mido," said Gavin. He knew his friend would again offer to help. He still wasn't sure how to respond.

They reached the bottom of the stairs and began following the crowd into the auditorium. Inside, they found three seats at the back. Gavin looked around. The auditorium was packed with students and teachers.

"Hey," said Mido, nudging him. "You want me to go up there?"

It was a tempting offer. Mido was good at public speaking. *But no one here knows us*, thought Gavin. *And if he goes up there, how will anyone know that it's my team and I'm the coach?*

He opened his mouth to speak. "I . . . I'll do it."

Mido looked surprised. "Okay. If you're sure."

A tall man in a grey suit walked across the stage at the front of the auditorium. He held the microphone stand with one hand and leaned in.

The Speech

"Good afternoon, ladies and gentlemen," boomed his deep voice through speakers on both sides of the auditorium. "Welcome to the start of another great year at Vandyke Secondary. We hope . . ."

Gavin stopped listening. His eyes focused on the microphone, then on the bright lights of the stage, and then his gaze swept across the huge sea of students. He felt sick to his stomach. Why had he declined Mido's offer? Was it too late to change his mind?

"Gav," whispered Critter, nudging his elbow, "you're up."

Gavin rose to his feet and walked forward. As he climbed the steps to the stage, he thought about a history book his mother had given him once. He hadn't read much of it, but he remembered the part about public executions in the Middle Ages. They were really gory, the kind where the axeman held up the head afterwards and the crowd cheered like crazy.

On the stage, Coach Sonderhoff was waiting next to the microphone.

You can do this, Gavin told himself. He stepped forward to the mic, opened his mouth to speak — and felt his foot slam against something hard.

He lurched forward, trying to catch the microphone stand as it wobbled. His hands closed on air. The stand clattered hard against the stage. Loud electronic shrieks echoed through the auditorium's sound system.

Out in the audience, students started giggling,

pointing, chattering. Gavin saw teachers trying to shush everyone, but it took a while for the noise to settle down.

Coach Sonderhoff rushed over to help pick up the microphone. When the auditorium was finally quiet, he gestured for Gavin to begin again.

Reaching into his pocket, Gavin found a crumpled sheet of paper. He fumbled with the paper for a moment, then mumbled, "First soccer practice is tomorrow after school."

Someone in the audience made a fart noise, followed by scattered applause and laughter.

Just like in the Middle Ages, thought Gavin, hurrying off the stage. Only this time, he'd put his own head on the block.

6 THE DREAM TEAM

Gavin slammed his schoolbag on the floor of the change room. "I can't believe Mr. Cowan kept us in after class. Especially today."

Across the room, Critter was pulling his blue goal-keeper's shirt over his head. "I know. He's so strict."

Gavin fumbled a bit as he hurriedly put on his shin pads, socks, and boots. "Come on," he said, tying up his laces. "Let's get out there!"

"Just a sec," said Critter. He reached into his bag and snatched up his goalkeeper gloves. "Okay, ready!"

Outside, the football team was warming up on the main field. As he and Critter jogged down the sidelines, Gavin tried counting all the orange helmets. He soon gave up.

"Why are there so many players in that sport?" he said to Critter.

"No idea," said his friend. "Sure hope there's enough guys left for our soccer team."

Gavin didn't reply. He was thinking about his

disastrous speech at the assembly. Would anyone even want to play for his team?

There was a loud crunch to their left. Gavin and Critter turned and saw Derek, the chunky red-haired kid from homeroom class, lying flat on the ground. He had been tackled hard by a huge eleventh-grader.

"Did you see that?" exclaimed Critter. He sounded impressed. "That guy absolutely flattened him!"

They reached the shed, and Gavin took out the key Coach Sonderhoff had given him. At first, the lock wouldn't open. Gavin jiggled the key around until he finally heard a click.

They stepped into the shed. Inside were canvas bins marked with big capital letters.

TRACK. LACROSSE. FIELD HOCKEY. FOOTBALL.

"There it is," said Critter.

SOCCER.

They looked inside. Six old beaten-up soccer balls in a mesh carrying bag. One pile of cracked multi-coloured mini-cones. Two sets of stained bibs, some blue, some pink.

"Wow," said Gavin, shaking his head.

Critter picked up the bibs and the bag of soccer

balls. "Come on," he said. "We can't do anything about it right now."

Gavin scooped up the cones and followed his friend out of the shed. He relocked the door. When they reached the end of the field, he caught his first glimpse of the soccer team.

The players were standing in a small circle, bending forward to stretch their hamstrings.

In the middle of the circle was Mido.

"Why's that one guy wearing jeans?" asked Critter.

"*Jeans?*" said Gavin, shocked. "Who wears jeans to soccer practice?" But as he looked around, he noticed that a few players were wearing long heavy cargo shorts, and at least two were wearing running shoes instead of soccer boots.

Mido ran over to Gavin.

"Hey, I wrote down everyone's names," he said, handing over a clipboard and pen. "We've only got twelve players, including you two, but that's still enough for a team and . . ."

He continued talking, but Gavin wasn't listening. He was too busy checking out the circle of players around him. Four small guys stood grouped together on the right, whispering nervously. Three of them were wearing glasses. Next to them stood a guy so skinny his legs looked like an insect's.

And, of course, there was the guy wearing jeans.

"Hey, aren't you the one who kicked over the

microphone?" said a voice to Gavin's right. A tough-looking guy with blond spiky hair stared back at him. He was tanned and wore two gold chains around his neck. "That was hilarious."

He coughed, then spat on the ground. "So," he said, "where's the coach?"

Gavin took a deep breath. "I'm the coach."

Every single pair of eyes seemed to fix on him at once. No one said a word. It was so quiet, Gavin could hear football pads crashing together in the distance.

"Okay," he said shakily. "I guess we should go for a run."

"We already ran," said the guy with the blond spiky hair.

"Yeah," the skinny guy said, "Blair's right. I joined this team to play soccer, not train for the Olympics."

Mido stepped forward. "Come on, guys. Gavin says run, so let's run."

Gavin shifted uneasily on his feet. The blond guy, Blair, and the skinny guy were still glaring at him.

"Th-that's okay," he said, taking the bag of soccer balls from Critter. "Let's do some passing."

"Can't we just play a game?" whined one of the four small guys, readjusting his glasses on his nose.

"Just pass for a little bit, okay?" said Gavin, empty-ing the mesh bag of balls on the ground.

Blair picked one up. He spun it around in his hands. "What the hell is this?" he demanded. He shoved the scruffy old ball into Gavin's arms.

"I'm sorry," said Gavin. "We haven't got anything else."

Blair snorted and snatched the ball away. The skinny guy followed him. The rest of the players drifted away with their partners.

Gavin joined up with Mido and Critter, and they found a free patch of ground. Mido sent over a soft pass. Just before it reached Gavin, the ball hit a hole in the ground and popped over his foot.

"That's our coach?" jeered someone behind him. "Nice skills."

Gavin felt like kicking himself. He'd wanted to make a good impression on these guys, wanted to show them he knew what he was doing. Now, it looked like he couldn't even control a simple pass. But after a few minutes of knocking the ball around with his friends, he started to relax and enjoy himself.

And then he remembered the rest of the team.

Turning around, he saw Jeans Guy standing by himself, rolling a ball backwards and forwards under his foot. The four little guys were diving around, trying to tackle each other. And on the far side of the field, the skinny guy was tossing the ball into the air while Blair flipped backwards, trying to do bicycle kicks.

"Want to call everyone in?" asked Mido, looking over in Blair's direction. "Looks like we need to explain things again."

Gavin nodded. "Everyone in!" he yelled.

The four little guys sprinted toward him, laughing and shoving. The other players jogged in quickly. Gavin was about to speak, but then noticed Blair and the skinny guy were still halfway across the field, ambling slowly toward the group.

"Hey!" shouted Mido. "Hurry up!"

The two boys ignored him.

"Yo, Coach," said Blair with a nasty smirk when he finally joined the group. "Game time?"

Gavin noticed Mido's fists were clenched.

"Sure," he said, shrugging. "Why not?"

He found the bag of bibs and began handing them out to divide the team up into Blues and Pinks. He gave Blair a pink bib and the skinny boy a blue one.

"Nah," said Blair, pointing to his friend. "Jamie's on my team."

"Fine, whatever," said Gavin, taking off his own blue bib and handing it to Blair. He avoided looking at Mido.

"We don't have any nets," someone mentioned.

Gavin hadn't thought about that. The rusty old goals leaning up against the fence looked big and hard to move. And anyway, they only had enough players for six a side.

"What about cones?" suggested Mido, holding up four pieces of the faded plastic.

Gavin nodded. He was annoyed he hadn't thought of that.

Once the cones were in place, marking out two goals, the game began. Gavin passed the ball to Mido, who knocked it out wide to Jeans Guy. The pass rebounded off his shin toward Blair.

Mido ran over to try to tackle him. Blair faked left, then slipped the ball between Mido's legs. He did a step-over fake and dribbled past one of the little guys. Then he chipped the ball up into the air and hammered it at the goal with his right foot. A lightning-quick arm from Critter tipped the ball around one of the cones.

The guy might be a jerk, thought Gavin, *but he's got skill*.

Because Critter had tipped the ball out, Blair took a corner kick. As the ball sailed in front of the goal, Gavin jumped to try to head it away.

Thump! Another head beat him to the ball, sending it hurtling toward the goal. Critter smothered the ball in his arms.

"Great header, Jamie," Blair called out. "Easy goal next time."

Gavin surged forward. His legs felt charged now, electrified by the competition. *I need a goal*, he told himself. *Right now*.

He controlled Critter's long throw on his thigh, then spun around, facing Blair. He faked left, but went right. He felt an elbow dig into his ribs but kept going. Pushing the ball forward, he smashed a shot past the small player in goal. It zipped between the two cones.

"Great goal!" shouted Mido.

That's more like it, thought Gavin.

He turned and saw Blair looking at him. But he couldn't read the expression on the blond player's face.

From the football field, they heard Coach Sonderhoff calling out to them.

"What's he saying?" asked Gavin.

Jeans Guy spoke up first. His voice was high and squeaky. "I think that's all for today, guys. Hey, when's our first game?"

7 THE KEY TO SUCCESS

Ever since Gavin's mother had enrolled in a weekly cooking class, dinner at home had become more and more adventurous. Gavin loved it all, from the homemade Russian borscht to the handmade Japanese sushi. Granddad had been a bit harder to convince.

That night, they were having an Indonesian curry with salad and rice.

Gavin watched Granddad from across the table. The old man was eyeing his plate with suspicion.

"What do you call this again?" he said, stirring the food with his fork.

"*Rendang* curry, Dad," replied Gavin's mother. "It's Indonesian."

"All right," said Granddad, taking a deep breath. "Here we go again, taste buds."

He tried a small spoonful. "Good lord, that's nice," he said, sounding surprised. Then he reached for his glass of water. "Even if it's hotter than the surface of the sun."

Gavin took a bite. The curry was hot, but delicious.

They all ate in silence for a while until Granddad spoke again. "So how did the football go, mate?"

"Not bad," Gavin mumbled. He was glad his mouth was full of food. He didn't want to admit that things hadn't exactly gone smoothly.

"He started the whole team himself, you know," said Granddad proudly to Gavin's mother and father. "And he's the coach."

"Granddad . . ." Gavin could feel his cheeks burning.

Gavin's father set down his glass. "Well, I think that's fantastic, Gavin. You started a whole *football* team yourself?"

Gavin shrugged. "I guess."

"That's wonderful too about the coaching," his father continued. "What great experience. What's the name of the teacher you're helping?"

"No, no," Granddad interrupted. "Gavin's the top man, the one in charge. The sports teacher who's sponsoring the team only understands that silly American type of football. Just like that ridiculous coach from the summer — O'Connor."

"Luckily, some of us know a bit more about real football," he added with a little grin. "Right, mate?"

"You're sure you're up to this, Gav?" asked Gavin's father.

Gavin spoke up. "It's no big deal, Dad. I'm just a player on the team, really."

"I don't know," said Gavin's mother, laying down her fork. "Couldn't coaching be a lot of extra work, Gavin? I mean, you're not in middle school anymore. I don't want you to fall behind in your classes."

"Your mother's right," Gavin's father agreed. "Don't forget that school comes first."

"It'll be *fine*," said Gavin. He finished what was left of his dinner. "May I be excused?"

His father nodded. "Put your dishes in the dishwasher."

Gavin took his plate into the kitchen. *Why are my parents always on my case about school?* he wondered. *I'm no Mido, but I always get As and Bs.*

But in the back of his mind was Mr. Cowan's math class.

★★★

The next practice was on Thursday afternoon. This time, Gavin and Critter persuaded their French teacher to let them out early.

"Madame LeBlanc rules," said Critter as they walked out to the field. "Even though I never understand anything she says. It's all in French."

As they jogged past the football uprights, he turned toward Gavin. "Hey, what's that position in American football where you run and catch the ball? Retriever?"

Gavin burst out laughing. "It's called receiver,

thickhead! A retriever is a kind of dog."

Critter grinned. "Bet I can catch way better than those guys."

"Way better," Gavin agreed.

When they got to the equipment shed, he put his hand into his right pocket. No key. Left pocket. No key.

"Gav?"

Gavin looked at his tall friend. "I must have left it in my bag."

He ran back to the locker room and emptied his bag. No key.

When he returned to the field, the football players had arrived. Some were putting on their orange helmets. Coach Sonderhoff was standing off to the side, writing on a clipboard.

Critter was waiting at the shed. The rest of the soccer team had gathered around him.

"Got the key, Gav?" asked Mido.

"No," said Gavin, shaking his head. "I must have dropped it."

"Well, I guess we could walk along in a line and search the grass," said Mido.

Gavin shrugged. He didn't have any better ideas.

As they formed a line and began searching, Gavin looked up and locked eyes with Coach Sonderhoff. The coach looked puzzled.

He doesn't know this sport, Gavin told himself. *Maybe he'll just think this is some strange soccer drill.*

"Got it!" shouted someone to his right.

Gavin spun around.

There it was, the key, dangling from a chubby finger. Derek, the red-haired guy from homeroom, grinned at Gavin.

"What are *you* doing here?" Gavin blurted out. As soon as he'd spoken, he wished he could take the words back. He hadn't meant to embarrass the guy in front of the whole team.

"I got cut from football," mumbled Derek, looking down at the ground. "I was hoping to try out for soccer."

Gavin started to reply, but then hesitated. Mido chimed in. "That's great," he said. "We only have one sub. We could use some more players."

Derek grinned again. "Oh good. Can I help get the equipment or something?"

"Sure," Gavin said.

Inside the shed, Gavin glanced over at Derek. *Doesn't look like much of a soccer player*, he thought. But he had to admit, Mido was right. They needed more players. They couldn't afford to be choosy.

Outside, the players did two quick warm-up laps around the field, then gathered around Gavin again.

What next? he wondered. Losing the key had really thrown him off. He couldn't seem to think straight. "Okay, so . . . get a partner. I mean . . . no, get in threes . . ."

"Can't we just play a game?" said Blair, his boot

resting on a soccer ball. "We already missed half the practice because you lost the key."

Mido spoke up. "Hey, wait a minute —"

"No, no, you're right," Gavin said firmly. "Let's have a game."

He grabbed the pile of blue and pink bibs and began passing them out.

Mido took his bib and walked away, shaking his head as he went.

Standing next to Gavin was Jeans Guy. He was wearing jeans again. Next to him stood Derek.

"Where do you play, Derek?" Gavin asked.

The big guy looked confused. "How about defence? Or maybe goalie?"

Critter was on the other team.

"Go in goal for now," said Gavin. *At least he'll fill up half the net*, he thought, a little guiltily.

"Hey, how come we've got all the shrimps?" complained Blair, pointing around at his team.

Gavin hadn't noticed. He'd put all four small guys on a team with Blair and Mido. "Oh, well, I guess we could switch —"

"The teams are fine," said Mido. "Ollie, Diego, Taiki, Mikey, you're with Blair and me."

It took Gavin a moment to realize who Mido was talking to. *Some coach I am*, he thought. *I don't even know my own players' names.*

"Hey," said Critter, shaking his head, "I can't tell

them apart. Let's call them the Tiny Giants."

That made Gavin feel a bit better.

The teams lined up. Mido kicked the ball to one of the Tiny Giants. It bounced over the small boy's foot and went out for a throw-in.

"Unlucky, unlucky!" called Mido, clapping his hands together. "Good effort."

"Effort doesn't matter if you suck," Gavin heard someone mutter. He turned and saw Blair strutting by.

Jeans Guy took the throw-in, but jumped as he threw the ball.

"Foul throw," sneered Blair. "Your feet need to stay on the ground, idiot. Our ball."

Gavin picked the ball up and tossed it to Blair.

"Why don't we let him try again?" said Mido. "This is practice, after all."

Blair snorted and threw the ball right over Mido's head.

One of the Tiny Giants tried to control it. The ball bounced off his shin pad back to Blair. The blond player chipped the ball up into the air with his right foot, then flicked it past Jeans Guy. Racing toward Derek's goal, he faked a hard shot, then slipped the ball through the chubby boy's legs.

"All day long," he crowed as he walked back.

Gavin took a pass from the skinny guy, Jamie. Pushing the ball forward, he sidestepped around Mido, then sprinted between two Tiny Giants. Critter came out to challenge the shot. Gavin curled the ball just out of the keeper's reach and just inside the left cone.

"Not bad," said Blair quietly as Gavin passed by. "But watch this."

Sprinting out to the right, Blair controlled a long throw from Critter on his chest. Gavin chased after him.

Blair beat one opposing player, then another, and then another. But just before he reached the front of the goal, Gavin caught up, blocking his way.

"Blair — over here!" someone yelled. It was Mido.

Blair ignored him and smashed a shot. It bounced off Gavin's shin and went wide of the goal.

Gavin heard Mido swearing as he ran to get the ball.

Mido's corner kick was a good one, sailing right in front of the goal. But Jamie jumped higher than everyone else and headed the ball away. Gavin gave chase, legs pumping. As he closed in on the goal, Critter charged. So instead of blasting a shot, Gavin opened his stance and tried to dribble around the keeper. Critter plunged and knocked the ball away with his fingers, but the ball rebounded off Gavin's shins and dribbled into the net.

Thud. Someone crashed hard into Gavin's shoulder, sending him tumbling to the ground.

"What the hell, man!"

Gavin rolled over just in time to see Mido shoving Blair hard in the chest.

Jamie ran over and grabbed Mido by the shirt. "Hey! What do you think you're doing?"

Gavin leaped to his feet. He saw Critter trying to pull Mido away.

"That was a cheap shot!" Mido raged. "What are you trying to do — injure your own teammate?"

"Calm down, man," said Critter, his arm around his friend.

"We can't just let him get away with that!" exclaimed Mido.

Gavin held up his hands. "Mido, I'm okay. See? Not injured."

"Everything all right over there, boys?" *Oh no*, thought Gavin. He turned around.

Coach Sonderhoff.

"We're about to call it quits over here," said the coach. "Maybe you'd better call it a day too."

The players were just starting to turn and walk off the field when Coach Sonderhoff spoke again. "Can I see you over here for a minute, Gavin?"

Gavin nodded weakly. He walked over to where Coach was standing.

"Everything okay with the team?" asked the big man, looking down at him.

Gavin looked down at the ground. "Yeah, it's fine, thanks. Coming along fine."

"Didn't look so fine just now," said Coach, nodding toward Critter's goal. "And what was with all of you searching the grass earlier on? Don't try to tell me that was some kind of soccer drill."

"It was nothing, Coach, really —"

"It had better be nothing," Coach Sonderhoff interrupted. "I told you when you started this team that it needs to be hassle-free for me. Players shoving around their own teammates is not hassle-free. You'd better make sure it doesn't happen again."

Gavin felt like he couldn't breathe.

"Oh yeah, and your first game is next Tuesday," said Coach. "Away, at St. Mike's."

8 LUNCH WITH THE ENEMY

Mido slammed his bottle of water down on the table. "He's such an idiot!"

"Whoa, chill, dude," said Critter. "You're scaring those nice old ladies."

Gavin looked behind Mido. A trio of elderly women were eyeing the boys and muttering among themselves.

Gavin turned back to his friends. Critter was munching a huge sandwich. Mido was glaring down at his bottle of water like it had done something to offend him.

"Too bad the English Premier League's on a break this week," said Critter, his mouth half full of sandwich. "I was looking forward to your grandfather's breakfast."

Gavin grinned. "He felt pretty bad about last weekend. He said he's going to make the sausages extra greasy next time to make up for it."

"Nice," said Critter. He leaned back, so that the front legs of his chair came up off the ground.

Without Soccer Saturday to wake up for that

morning, Gavin had slept until eleven. After that, he'd come to the mall to meet Mido and Critter.

"You know, I slept seventeen hours last night," said Critter. He yawned. "But I'm still a bit sleepy."

Mido spoke up. "Gavin, what are we going to do about that Blair guy on the soccer team?"

Gavin took a sip from his drink. He shrugged. "What do you mean?"

Mido held up his hands. "What do you think I mean? He mouths off to everyone, he doesn't pass, and he blindsided you last practice."

"I still managed to score past Critter," said Gavin.

"Yeah, with your shin pad," laughed his tall friend. He took a friendly swipe at Gavin, who ducked.

"I'm just saying," Mido went on, "maybe the team's better off without him."

Gavin turned toward him. He was starting to get annoyed. "We've only got thirteen players, Mido. Four are the size of Critter's little brother. One's shaped like a sumo wrestler. And one wears jeans to practice! Blair can actually play. What do you want me to do? Cut one of our only good players?"

"Okay, okay," said Mido, holding out his hands. "I'm just saying that the guy plays for himself — no one else. Forget it."

Critter leaned further back in his chair. "Hey guys, check that out."

Gavin glanced in the direction Critter was looking.

Three pretty girls were walking arm in arm through the middle of the food court.

Critter's chair fell backward and hit the floor hard. The sound echoed around the food court. Everyone turned to see what had happened, including the trio of girls.

The elderly ladies behind Mido stood up to leave. Gavin saw one of them shoot Critter a nasty look.

"Aw, man, look at my sandwich." Somehow Critter had managed to jump free of the falling chair. His sandwich hadn't been so lucky; it was now a jumble of bread, chicken, and lettuce on the floor.

"Shouldn't be too hard to score on a goalkeeper who can't even sit in a chair."

Gavin looked up.

It was Craig, their old middle-school teammate. His jacket said St. Michael's on the front. Behind him stood four tall guys, all wearing similar jackets.

Gavin stood up. "You guys call each other this morning for clothing advice?"

One of the St. Michael's guys pointed a long finger at Gavin. He turned toward Craig. "This the guy you've been talking about, Sniper?"

"*Sniper?*" laughed Gavin. He pointed at Craig. "This guy? He's the reason we didn't win summer league this year."

Craig glanced around nervously for a moment, then turned back to Gavin. "You never passed," he sneered.

"Not my fault you're a ball hog. Anyway —" he said, gesturing toward Gavin and his two friends "— who'd ever listen to these guys talking about soccer? They play for Vandyke!"

"Not tough enough to make the football team, I guess, huh?" said one of the St. Mike's players.

"Do you even use a ball at practices?" asked Craig.

What a stupid thing to say, thought Gavin. But then he remembered the ratty old soccer balls in the Vandyke sports shed. Craig wasn't far off. And that hurt.

"And what's this I hear about you — *you!* — coaching?" Craig said. He held up his hands. "What are we gonna do, guys? Gavin's the coach. We've only got Coach DeJong. He only played for the Canadian national team fifty times —"

The St. Mike's players all dissolved into laughter.

He played for the national team fifty times? thought Gavin, feeling panic rise in his chest. *I'm just a kid. How can I compete with that?*

"What's in there, Craig?" said Critter, pointing at the plastic bag in Craig's hand.

Craig held the bag out toward them. SOCCER PLUS was printed across the front.

"New Predator boots, boys," he said. "We all have 'em."

His teammates nodded.

Jeans Guy flashed into Gavin's mind. Then the pink bibs. Then the battered cones.

"No boots in the world can make you *not* suck at soccer, Craig," said Critter. "Even if they kicked the ball for you."

The biggest St. Mike's player took a step toward Critter, but Craig held out a hand to stop him.

"We'll see these losers Tuesday," he said, his smug grin spreading wider. "If they actually bother to show up. Not that there's much point."

★★★

When Gavin got home, he found his mother in the small room at the little desk where she liked to work. Her black-rimmed reading glasses were perched low on her nose. She was peering into a thick book while typing into her computer.

"Hey buddy," she said, glancing up.

"Hi Mom," he said. "Where's Granddad?"

"He went upstairs to lie down," she replied. "Got a touch of cold, I think."

Gavin's thoughts turned to the game on Tuesday. What if Granddad couldn't come?

From the kitchen came the sound of a whistling kettle.

Gavin's mother stood up. "Actually, I was just making him some tea. Shall we go up and see how he's doing?"

In the kitchen, she prepared the tea and then

handed Gavin a plate of cookies. They climbed the stairs together. Gavin's grandfather's bedroom was the first room on the left. The door was open.

"Hello, mate," said Granddad as they entered the room. "Ah, cheers for the tea, Kathy."

He was lying with his head propped up by some pillows. A newspaper lay spread out on his lap. He coughed as Gavin passed him the plate of cookies.

"You all right, Granddad?" asked Gavin.

"Thanks, m'boy," replied Granddad. "And yes, not to worry. I'll be right as rain in a day or two."

Gavin's mother placed his cup of tea on a table next to the bed. "Here you are, Dad," she said. "Careful now. That tea's hot."

"I should hope so," said Granddad. "I don't much care for cold tea."

Gavin's mother rolled her eyes. "I guess I'll leave you two gents alone to chat."

She walked out of the room.

"Biscuit?" said Gavin's grandfather, tossing a cookie at Gavin.

Gavin caught it, then sat down in the big armchair next to the window. He examined the cookie in his hand. It looked like cardboard. He took a bite. Cardboard.

"Why do you always eat these, Granddad?" he asked.

Gavin's grandfather chuckled. "I don't know. They're not very nice, are they? I guess they remind me of when I was a lad in England. So much of the food was rubbish back then."

"So you miss bad food?" asked Gavin, confused.

"Well, not exactly," laughed Gavin's grandfather. "But I guess eating these biscuits makes me remember those days a bit. You see, we lived in a small village outside Ipswich. Everyone knew everyone there. After we started up our football team, we started playing against the villages and towns around us."

"Did you beat them?" asked Gavin.

"When we didn't, we were very disappointed," said his grandfather. "It sounds silly now, but they were the enemy to us."

Gavin thought about Craig and the other St. Mike's guys in the mall.

"There was one game I've never forgotten," continued Gavin's grandfather. "It was halftime in a very rough cup game against a team from the village next to ours. We were losing 2–0. Two of our lads had already been red-carded and kicked out, so we were down to nine players. We all came into the dressing room raging about the referee and the dirty way the other team was playing. Pretty soon we started blaming one another. All of a sudden there was an earsplitting crack against the wall behind us. It was the old gaffer, his face scarlet red. His walking stick had shattered in two and he was pointing at the wall.

"'Look at yourselves,' he said, 'acting like a pack

of bloody animals. Those guys in that other room are laughing right now, because they've gotten to you. They've got you fighting with the referee, with them, with each other. They've got you focused on everything except actually playing football.'"

"What happened next?" asked Gavin.

"Well," his grandfather replied, "we didn't win. But at the end, the score was 2–2. And boy, did it ever feel like a victory."

9 A PACK OF ANIMALS

"Arrgh — I can't believe how much homework I got today," groaned Mido, setting his soccer bag down on the change room floor.

"Tell me about it," said Critter. "It's like the teachers at this school are out to get us, eh, Gav?"

"What?" said Gavin. He hadn't been listening. All he could think about was the game.

First game of the season. First game for his new team. First game as coach.

He was already sweating. And they hadn't even started the warm-up.

"School work," repeated Mido slowly, as if speaking to a small child. "Today. Lots of it."

"Oh, yeah," Gavin mumbled. The school day seemed like a blur to him now, but he did remember there had been a lot of homework assigned.

He looked around the change room. The four Tiny Giants sat together in one corner, getting undressed and talking in low voices. Blair was down at the far end of the room, a pair of big white headphones on his head. Jamie sat next to him, fiddling around with his phone.

Jeans Guy was standing in the middle of the room. He was once again wearing jeans. "Do y–you have the uniforms, Coach?" he stammered.

It took Gavin a moment to realize the guy was talking to him. "Yeah," he said. He unzipped the big black bag that Coach Sonderhoff had given to him earlier that day. "Here they are."

A jumble of orange-and-black fabric tumbled onto the floor.

"You can't be serious," said Mido, holding up a pair of bright orange shorts. He tried them on. Even on Mido, they were pretty short.

The jerseys had vertical orange and black stripes, and a tiger crest. Gavin pulled one on over his head. It was tight and uncomfortable.

Coach Sonderhoff walked into the room. "I think the referee wants to start soon," he said. "You almost ready?"

Gavin nodded. The big man left the room.

"Listen up, guys," said Gavin.

No one paid any attention. The Tiny Giants kept talking, Jamie kept texting, and Blair kept bobbing his head to the music on his headphones.

"Let's just get out there," Gavin said, hoping they'd all heard him. He finished tying his left boot, then stood and headed outside. The rest of the team followed.

A Pack of Animals

In the twenty minutes since the Vandyke players had arrived at St. Michael's Academy, a large crowd had gathered to watch the game.

"Look at them all," muttered Mido as he walked out onto the field next to Gavin.

The St. Michael's Stallions were warming up down at the far end. They wore white shirts, black shorts, and black socks. Gavin caught sight of Craig leading the warm-up. He clenched his fists.

The referee walked over to Gavin, whistle between his teeth. "Time to get started, Coach. You ready to go?"

"What about our warm-up?" asked Gavin.

The referee shook his head. He pointed to the sidelines. "Coach DeJong says we've got to get started."

Gavin looked over and saw a short muscular man in a black-and-white track suit. The man was barking instructions at the St. Mike's players like a drill sergeant.

"Hey, guys," called Gavin. "Everyone in. We're starting right away."

Mido had already begun kicking a ball at Critter. He walked over to Gavin, hands raised in disbelief. "Hey, what's going on? Don't we get to warm up?"

Gavin shrugged. "I guess not."

"That isn't fair," said Mido. "Go tell Coach Sonderhoff."

Gavin glanced over at Coach Sonderhoff. The big man was sitting in the back of the bleachers, reading a book. Gavin remembered what he'd said: If the soccer team became a hassle, there wouldn't be a soccer team anymore.

"Come on, Meeds," he said. "Let's just get on with it."

"But it's not —"

Three blasts from the referee's whistle cut Mido short.

"Okay, well, Critter in goal," began Gavin. He went through the rest of the starting lineup, leaving Derek and Jeans Guy on the bench.

"Okay, well, let's get out there," he added. *Not exactly the most inspiring pre-game speech*, he thought.

Gavin recognized the two men sitting right in front of Coach Sonderhoff. That jacket and cap could belong to only one person — his grandfather. The old man was sitting next to Gavin's father. Nervous energy surged into Gavin's muscles. *I can't let Granddad down*, he thought. *And I need to prove to Dad that being a coach is worth it.*

The Stallions won the coin toss and chose first ball. At the halfway line, a tall muscular guy with a shaved head stared back at Gavin.

"Nice uniforms," he smirked.

Craig was standing behind the tall guy. "Did you borrow them from the cheerleaders?" he jeered.

Gavin said nothing. He just glared back at them.

Tweeeee! The referee blew a long blast on his whistle. Craig tapped the ball sideways.

The skinhead striker dribbled forward. Blair made a half-hearted attempt to tackle. The striker stepped around him easily.

"Come on, Blair, put a foot in!" yelled Mido.

The striker slipped easily past two Tiny Giants. He smashed a shot from just outside the box. It sailed toward the bottom right corner. Critter dove, stretching out one of his octopus arms, just managing to tip the ball around the post.

Gavin decided to stay up front during the St. Mike's corner kick. He knew it was important that one striker stayed up there to pounce on any quick counterattack chances.

"Blair!" roared Mido. "Get back and defend!"

It was then that Gavin noticed Blair standing a few metres to his left. The blond boy shrugged in Mido's direction, then pointed at Gavin. "Why me? Why not him?"

"Come on, dude, get back there," said Gavin.

Blair took a few reluctant steps back toward goal, then stopped.

The corner kick sailed into the penalty area. Critter leaped into the air. The lanky goalkeeper's fist met with the ball and the bald Stallions striker's elbow met with his face.

Critter collapsed in a heap on the ground.

Gavin sprinted back just in time to see Mido shove the bald striker to the ground.

"What the hell, man?" Mido hollered.

The referee gave Mido a yellow card. "You're lucky to still be on the field, young man," he warned.

"What about the other guy, ref?" asked Gavin. "And what about that foul on our keeper?"

The referee ignored him.

"Yeah, ref!" exclaimed Mido.

"Forget it," Gavin told him. The yellow card was just a warning. But if there was any more rough stuff or problems with the referee, Mido might get a red card and be kicked out of the game.

Critter rose groggily to his feet. "I'm okay, guys."

The game restarted with a St. Michael's throw-in. It landed at Craig's feet. Gavin lunged at him and won the ball cleanly. Craig flopped down on the ground, clutching his ankle.

Tweeeee!

Craig placed the ball on the ground. He winked at Gavin. His ankle didn't seem too badly injured.

Gavin heard some of the St. Mike's fans on the sidelines, laughing behind him.

"That was a dive!" he complained.

The ref ran over and gave Gavin a yellow card. Gavin threw his hands up in the air. Now he and Mido were both living dangerously.

The free kick floated into the area. Critter loped forward for the easy catch. "Keeper!" he shouted, warning his teammates to get out of the way.

But Mido had already leaped to head the ball away.

Distracted by Critter's shout, he lost his concentration. The ball skimmed off the back of his head and landed in the Vandyke net.

Mido put his hands over his face. *He'd scored an own goal.*

Critter was left standing there, stunned.

Behind the goal, St. Mike's fans erupted into cheers and hoots of laughter.

Back at centre, Gavin kicked the ball to Blair. The blond striker skipped past Craig, did a spin move around a defender, then raced down the left wing.

Gavin spotted Mido sprinting toward the far post. "Send it across!" he was yelling.

Blair looked up. But instead of crossing the ball to Mido, he tried to dribble past a defender. This time, the defender tackled the ball away.

St. Mike's counterattacked quickly. Their right midfielder send a long ball forward. The skinhead striker smashed it out of mid-air. Critter saved. Craig tapped in the rebound for an easy goal.

"Blair, I was wide open!" Mido shouted.

Blair ignored him. He jogged back toward centre. He didn't seem worried at all that he'd cost them a goal.

Gavin booted a clump of dirt.

The rest of the first half was a nightmare for the Tigers. Passes bounced off shin pads, free kicks kept going to the Stallions, and Mido got angrier and angrier at Blair.

Gavin had the Tigers' only shot. It was from a long way out and sailed high over the Stallions' net.

When the halftime whistle went, it was 3–0 for St. Mike's.

As soon as the Vandyke team got to the side of the field, Mido turned on Blair. "Why don't you learn how to pass?" he snapped. "It's not a one-man game."

Blair poked Mido in the chest.

"Just 'cause I'm better than you," he said, an arrogant smirk on his face. "And anyway, it seems like you're better at scoring on your own net."

Mido moved to take a swing at the grinning blond striker. Critter caught his arm just in time.

"Why are you all taking this so seriously?" said Jeans Guy. "I thought we were out here to have fun."

"Yeah — losing's really fun," snapped Jamie. "That's the stupidest thing I ever heard."

Gavin caught a glimpse of Granddad, sitting in the stands. The old man was frowning and shaking his head.

Look at us, thought Gavin. *Fighting amongst ourselves. Like a pack of animals.*

"Come on, guys," said Gavin. He couldn't think of anything else to say.

As the teams jogged back onto the field, Mido ran up beside Gavin. "Gav, you've got to take Blair off."

"What do you want me to do? Put in those two?" said Gavin, pointing at Derek and Jeans Guy.

"At least they might put in some effort. And pass.

That idiot never stops hogging the ball!"

"Why can't you just . . . leave it?" said Gavin. And before Mido could say anything else, he turned and walked away.

From the restart, Blair took the ball again and danced through the St. Michael's midfield. Craig tried to tackle him and missed, tumbling awkwardly to the ground.

"Hey!" shouted Gavin, sprinting into an opening. "Over here!"

Blair saw Gavin, but swivelled and shot instead. The ball left his boot and soared past the keeper's fingertips.

Clang! It rebounded off the crossbar. The ball landed at Gavin's feet. He passed it easily into the net.

Blair jogged over and high-fived him, coolly. "Nice one."

Some of the Vandyke players joined them. Mido did not.

The comeback was short-lived.

Once more, the Stallions got a corner kick. Once more, Mido hollered at Blair to get back and help defend. Once more, Blair refused. And once more, the skinhead striker elbowed Critter. This time, he got his head to the ball and it rolled into the back of the net.

The Tigers complained to the referee. He ignored them and pointed to centre. 4–1 Stallions.

The last kick of the game was a cross from Jamie. It soared over Gavin's head and went out for a Stallions goal kick.

The referee blew his whistle three times.

Gavin stared upward into the grey September sky. *What a disaster.* He looked over at his father and Granddad. *I wish they hadn't seen this.*

All around the field, St. Mike's fans were celebrating and poking fun at the Vandyke players.

"Nice coaching," mocked Craig as he walked past. "You guys suck so much we hardly needed to try. You beat yourselves for us."

10 TESTS AND PROMISES

The next day, Gavin was sitting at his desk, staring at a math quiz.

The last question was a big tangled equation with lots of letters and numbers.

He tried to answer it. Nothing. He tried another way. Nothing.

Setting down his pencil, he stared out the window. He let out a loud yawn, then froze.

Mr. Cowan was staring right at him. "Is this quiz too easy for you, Gavin?"

Gavin shook his head. He snatched up his pencil again.

He'd meant to study for this quiz. He really had. Last night, after dinner, he'd even sat down on his bed and opened up his textbook.

But sitting there in his bedroom, all Gavin had been able to think about was the game against St. Mike's. Mido and Blair bickering. The bald striker scoring. Craig sneering and gloating.

And so the textbook had stayed open, but unread.

"Time's up," said Mr. Cowan. "Pencils down, please."

He began to circle the room and collect the students' work. As Gavin handed over his quiz, he saw the teacher look at it and frown. Gavin cringed. He felt like a criminal who'd just signed a confession.

"Wow, did I ever bomb on that quiz," said Critter as they left the classroom.

"Tell me about it," said Gavin. He opened his locker and shoved his books inside.

"Yeah, right," replied Critter. "You, bombing on a math quiz? You always pass."

Gavin slammed his locker shut, then slung his backpack over his shoulder. "Well, I'm pretty sure that one was a disaster."

"Hey guys," said Mido, strolling up beside them. "How was the quiz?"

"Don't ask," said Critter.

"Hey Gavin. I mean, Coach."

Gavin looked up. The four Tiny Giants were passing by. The tallest one was giving him a thumbs-up.

"What's up, Coach?" said one of the other Giants.

"You see that?" said Gavin, after they'd walked away. "They called me Coach. Even after we lost the game."

Mido spoke up. "Well, maybe you impressed them. You did score a goal."

Yeah, thought Gavin, feeling a bit better. *I did. Maybe I'm not such a bad coach.*

"Yo, Coach G," said Critter. "When do we play St. Mike's again?"

"Let me think . . ." replied Gavin, trying to remember. "We play Templeton tomorrow, and then —"

"Two more games," Mido chimed in. "Templeton, Cedars, and then, if we win those two games, we get another chance against St. Mike's in the city final."

"Sounds good," said Critter, pounding his fist against his palm. "I want a rematch with that bald guy."

Gavin knew it wasn't fair, but he felt annoyed with Mido for remembering the schedule. *I'm the coach*, he told himself. *I should know when we play.*

The three friends reached the bottom of the stairs.

"I'll see you guys later," said Critter. He turned away.

"Where you going?" asked Gavin.

Critter shrugged. "To the gym. Coach Sonderhoff asked me to come see him. Don't know why. Hope I'm not in trouble."

"All right, catch you later," said Mido.

"Big game tomorrow," Critter called over his shoulder. "You two better be ready."

When Gavin and Mido got outside, the sky was grey and a light rain had begun to fall.

"Could be a muddy game tomorrow," said Gavin as they walked down the school steps.

Mido didn't reply.

"I sure hope we can win this one," Gavin went on.

Mido nodded, but still said nothing.

They continued walking, but it wasn't until they had left the school grounds that Mido finally spoke.

"Gav," he said calmly, "I'm sorry to say this. But as your friend, I feel I should tell you that you've got to be stronger as a coach. I mean, you let that Blair guy walk all over you."

Gavin looked down at the ground. "Well, I mean . . . that's not true," he mumbled.

Mido's voice rose in frustration. "Oh, come on, Gavin. He doesn't pass. He doesn't come back and defend. He listens to his headphones when you're trying to talk to the team . . ."

He trailed off.

Gavin didn't know what to say. Blair had skill. A lot of skill. But everything Mido was saying was also true.

"So what do you think I should do?" he said.

"Bench him!" said Mido. "It's the only way he'll get the message."

Am I running this team, thought Gavin, *or is Mido?*

★★★

"Earth to Gavin."

A bowl of spaghetti and meat sauce seemed to be hovering in mid-air. Gavin blinked.

"Sorry, Mom," he said, taking the bowl from her.

"What's with you?" she said. "It's like you're on another planet tonight."

Granddad spoke up. "How's the team looking for the game tomorrow, Gav?"

"I'm not sure," said Gavin, shrugging. He rolled some spaghetti on to his fork.

"Aha," said his mother. "Planet Soccer. I thought so."

The front door slammed shut in the other room. Gavin's father walked in.

"Hi honey," said Gavin's mother. "How was work?"

"Mmm, heavy day," he said, removing his jacket. "That conference next month just keeps getting bigger."

"And," he added, shooting a meaningful look Gavin's way, "there were a few extra problems."

He turned to Gavin's mother. "How was your day?"

She sighed. "The book's going to the publisher next week," she said. "So, yeah, busy times in our office, too."

Just as Gavin's father sat down, there were two harsh coughs from the other side of the table.

Gavin looked over at Granddad. The old man held his hands over his mouth and coughed twice more.

"You okay there, Dad?" said Gavin's mother.

"Still a touch of that cold," he replied. "All the same, would you mind very much if I went and had a little lie-down? Rude of me, but —"

"You sure you're all right?" Gavin's mother said.

"Yes, yes. Not to worry." He stood up. "Just need to recharge my batteries." He sent a half-smile in Gavin's direction.

Gavin watched as his mother got to her feet and followed the old man out of the room. They'd been gone only a moment when Gavin's father spoke.

"Seems like you and I need to have a little talk, Gavin."

Gavin knew that tone of voice. It was too soft. Too calm. Too measured. He was in trouble. But he couldn't imagine why.

"How's math class going, Gavin?" His father twirled a fork through his spaghetti.

Gavin nearly knocked over his glass of water, but caught it just in time.

"Just fine," he lied.

Gavin's father stopped twirling his fork and put it down on his plate. "That's not what I hear from Mr. Cowan."

Gavin's mother came back into the room. "What's going on?"

"I got an email this evening from Mr. Cowan, Gavin's math teacher. It seems that our son hasn't been keeping up with his homework," said Gavin's father. "Although, according to Gavin, everything's going just fine."

She turned to Gavin. "Is this true?"

Gavin nodded. He could feel a lump rising in his throat.

"You know that's not acceptable," said his mother.

Gavin's father sat back in his chair. He held out his

hands. "Look, son, we know high school's a big change. And you've had a lot on your plate with this soccer team and everything. But school comes first. If you're going to play sports, you need to keep up with your school work."

Gavin's heart seemed to fall into a deep pit in his stomach.

"Mr. Cowan told me there's another quiz this Friday," continued Gavin's father. "He said it's on everything you've studied over the first couple of weeks. And so from now until Friday, it's you and the math textbook, my friend. You'll go to Mr. Cowan's room after school tomorrow for some help catching up."

"But the game's tomorrow!" cried Gavin. He leaped up. "I'm the coach. I can't just miss the game."

"I know soccer means a lot to you," said his father. "But you've got to —"

"Mom!" cried Gavin. "Tell him this isn't fair!"

But his mother shook her head. "I'm sorry, Gavin. I agree with your father. School comes first."

11 THE SCRAPBOOK

"This *sucks!*" Gavin groaned. He kicked his locker. The loud bang echoed down the hallway.

A teacher opened her classroom door. She looked at Gavin, who was standing with Critter and Mido. "Everything all right?"

"Yeah, Miss Mitchell," replied Critter. "Everything's cool."

When she'd disappeared back into her room, he turned to Gavin. "I can't *believe* you're not playing today. It's so unfair."

"What are we going to do for strikers?" said Mido. "You're out, and Blair's —"

"Just play him, Mido," snapped Gavin. "We need to win this game, or we've got no chance of making the city final."

He saw the Tiny Giants walking toward them from the other end of the hallway. Derek was bumbling along with them. Gavin looked down at the math textbook in his hand and swore under his breath.

"So, Gavin, shall we get started?"

Gavin looked up and saw Mr. Cowan standing in the doorway to his classroom.

"I guess so," he mumbled. He turned to his friends. "Good luck, guys."

As he turned to follow Mr. Cowan through the doorway, Gavin felt a pat on his back. "Don't worry," said Critter behind him. "We'll win this one for you, Coach G."

Inside the classroom, Gavin stood watching as Mr. Cowan erased the whiteboard. He wasn't sure where he was supposed to sit. He'd never been in a room full of empty desks before.

I've never missed a soccer game in my whole life, he realized bitterly. *Not for injuries. Not for the flu. Not for any reason.*

"Thanks for coming, Gavin," said Mr. Cowan.

As if I have a choice, thought Gavin.

Mr. Cowan handed him a blue marker pen. "I thought we could do the questions from the last quiz on the board together. That way, I can see where you're going wrong and help you out."

Gavin sighed. He looked at the sheet of paper. It was a fresh copy of the last quiz.

"Do I really have to do this all again?" he asked. He knew that right now his friends would be boarding the bus for the trip across town to Templeton.

His teacher frowned. "Gavin, if you don't want this

extra help, I do have other things I could be doing."

So do I, thought Gavin. But he kept his mouth shut. He knew the only answer to the question. "Sorry, Mr. Cowan. I do want your help."

"That's better," said his teacher. "Okay, problems one to five — go for it!"

Stop trying to make this sound exciting, thought Gavin. He started copying out the problems. *Why would anyone ever want to be a teacher?* he wondered. *Especially a math teacher.*

He spent a few minutes trying to solve the problems. The first three were okay, but he got stuck on the last two.

"Good job," said Mr. Cowan, standing up from his desk. He walked over and wrote in a couple of numbers and symbols in red marker pen. "See how it works?"

Gavin looked. Then he nodded. "I can't believe I forgot to do that."

"Sometimes it takes just one little change to make things right," said Mr. Cowan. "Same as in soccer, right?"

For what seemed like hours, they continued. Gavin worked out the solutions. Mr. Cowan corrected him when he went wrong.

"Excellent!" exclaimed Gavin's teacher as he checked the final problem. "Good job — that was a tough one. You see, Gavin? You can do this stuff."

Gavin put down his marker. "Can I go now?"

Mr. Cowan nodded. "Yes, you can go. Just spend a

bit of time tonight on review questions."

Gavin picked up his backpack and started walking away.

"Hey," said Mr. Cowan, just before he reached the door. "I'm sorry you missed your game today."

Gavin forced a smile. "That's okay. See you tomorrow, Mr. Cowan."

Huh, thought Gavin. *He says sorry, and it's all supposed to be just fine?* But as he left the room, Gavin couldn't stop thinking about what his teacher had said. *Sometimes it takes just one little change to make things right.*

At home, Gavin found Granddad sitting in the old brown chair in the living room. He had a woolly blanket tucked around his knees. The steaming cup of tea in his hands wobbled a little as he lifted it to his lips.

"All right, mate?" he said.

With a groan, Gavin dropped his bag. He slumped down onto the couch.

"Guess not," said Granddad.

Gavin stared blankly at the television. Granddad was watching one of those English detective dramas he liked. Gavin didn't think much of them. They looked like they'd been filmed in the 1400s.

As if reading his thoughts, Granddad clicked the remote and switched off the television.

"Oy," he said, gesturing with both hands. "Come here a sec, m'boy."

Gavin scooted down to the other end of the couch.

He saw Granddad reach down next to his armchair and pick up something from the floor.

It was a large brown book. The cover was tattered and ripped, and the pages were yellowed with age.

His grandfather opened to the first page. "I've been meaning to show you this for a long time."

With everything that had happened in the past two days, Gavin wasn't exactly in the mood to look at another book. But it was Granddad, so he didn't say anything.

And then Gavin saw a single word, scrawled in messy handwriting across the first page.

Football.

Granddad flipped to the next page. There was an old newspaper article, protected under a thin plastic sheet. At the top of the article was a black-and-white photograph of a soccer team.

Gavin studied the players closely. They were all scowling at the camera. Their shirts looked heavy, with long sleeves and large collars. Their boots were big and bulky, like Gavin's hiking boots. Two players had impressive moustaches.

"Granddad," Gavin exclaimed. "It's you!"

He pointed to a player in the front row.

Granddad took a sip of his tea, then smiled. "Indeed it is. That was my debut match for the first team."

Gavin studied the photograph again. "You had hair!"

Granddad chuckled. "I was seventeen. Just a few years older than you."

"Says here," said Gavin, "that you lost the match 7–0?"

Granddad grimaced. "We were a disorganized rabble," he said. "Luckily the gaffer sorted us out soon enough."

Gavin pointed to the player kneeling next to Granddad in the photo. "Who's that?" The man had fierce eyes and a strange mop-like haircut.

"Ah," said Granddad with a faraway smile. "I hadn't thought about him in years. We called him Dizzy Deano."

"Dizzy Deano?" exclaimed Gavin. "What kind of a name is that?"

His grandfather looked at the photograph and chuckled. "He was a right nutter — a madman on the pitch. Tackled like a maniac."

"Doesn't sound like the nicest guy," said Gavin.

Granddad smiled again. "He was my best mate. Funniest lad on the team, a real joker. We were at school together from when we were little."

Gavin thought for a moment. "Was he any good at soccer?"

"He was solid," said Granddad, taking a sip of his tea. "Problem was, at the start of that season, he kept getting kicked out of games, you know? He always let his temper get the best of him."

"So what happened?" asked Gavin. "Did the gaffer bop him on the nose?"

Granddad nibbled a cookie, then continued. "Actually, I remember being quite surprised at what the gaffer did. It was after our third match — we'd just lost 4–1, and Deano'd been sent off for the third time in a row."

"That's quite a record," said Gavin. "Three for three."

Granddad smiled. "Indeed. Anyway, after that match, the old gaffer called me into his office. I followed him in, knees knocking together. I was only seventeen, re-member, and I was pretty terrified of this man. But what he said . . . well, it was the most surprising thing."

"What was it?" asked Gavin eagerly.

"He said to me, 'What do you think I should do about your mate Deano?' I still remember his steely grey eyes staring at me. Like they were burning a hole right through me.

"At first I told him I didn't know," Granddad con-tinued. "'Hogwash!' the gaffer snarled back at me. 'C'mon, boy — tell me what you think.'"

"What did you say?" asked Gavin.

"Well, he was ready to boot Deano right off the team," replied Granddad. "I told him I didn't think that was necessary, that Deano was a good lad. The gaffer said that wasn't acceptable, that he had to do something. And so I came up with a plan. I said that maybe sitting Deano out for a couple of matches would make him change."

"But he was your friend!" Gavin protested. He couldn't believe Granddad would go behind a friend's back like that.

Granddad sighed. "I know, I know. I sometimes still feel ashamed. But you know what? It worked. Deano hated missing the two games, and we lost both. I think he saw how much the team missed him and realized that when he got sent off, it was the same situation. He was being selfish. When he came back, he was a changed player. That was when we started to win."

Gavin saw a fierce-looking man in a suit standing behind the team in the photograph. "Is that the gaffer?" The guy didn't look like a coach. He looked more like an axe murderer.

Granddad nodded. "Understand now why my knees were quaking?"

"I'm surprised he asked your opinion," said Gavin.

"Me too," said Granddad. "Coaches back then weren't known for that sort of thing. But the gaffer did ask us now and then, quietly. He was pretty scary. But I guess deep down he was the sort of coach who valued the opinions of others, and knew how to get the most out of every player, even the difficult ones."

Gavin felt his phone buzzing in his pocket. "Just a second, Granddad."

He took the phone out and looked at the screen. Mido.

The game, thought Gavin.

He picked up the phone. "Hello?"

Mido was speaking so fast Gavin could barely keep up.

"Yup," he said into the phone. "Wow . . . Yup . . . Wow."

He put down the phone.

"What happened?" asked Granddad.

"We beat Templeton 3–0," said Gavin. He couldn't decide whether to cheer or curse. The Tigers had won, but they'd done it without him. Maybe they were better off without him, especially as coach.

His grandfather's face lit up. "Brilliant!" He looked at Gavin. "Oy, mate — maybe you should go study a little. Don't want to miss the next match, right?"

Gavin nodded reluctantly. He thought about Dizzy Deano. Missing a match really was the worst thing in the world.

Granddad closed the cover of the tattered old book and held it toward Gavin. "I'd like you to have this, mate."

12 RETURN OF THE COACH

"You should've seen the guys after we won," whispered Mido. "Everyone was so pumped up!"

"Yeah, you told me," replied Gavin. All weekend, Mido had gone on and on about the Templeton game. It was now Monday afternoon, and Gavin was sick of hearing about it.

"That'll never work," said Critter softly.

Gavin looked up. At the front of the room, their frizzy-haired science teacher was trying to light a piece of metal on fire.

Whoosh! The metal strip in his hand burst into bright white flames.

"Behold the amazing properties of magnesium!" announced the teacher grandly.

"Sweet!" said Critter, eyes wide. He nudged Gavin. "Check that out — his hand's on fire."

Gavin couldn't even force a half-smile. He had other things on his mind. Like the game after school. If the Tigers wanted another go at St. Mike's in the city final, they had to win today.

He thought about the last game. Why had the team won with Mido in charge and lost with *him?* Was it luck? Or was Mido a better coach?

The bell rang. Critter and Mido jumped out of their seats. Gavin dragged himself up on to his feet.

He'd been so distracted thinking about Mido and the game he'd almost forgotten that he still might not be playing. He needed to speak to Mr. Cowan first.

On the way to the math teacher's room, a feeling of doom churned in his stomach.

"Hi Gavin," said Mr. Cowan, waving him in. "I was just on the phone with your father."

Gavin's heart dropped into his shoes.

Mr. Cowan held up his test paper. "I knew you could do it."

At the top of the paper was a big red *A*.

Gavin froze in the doorway for a moment, then leaped into the air. "Yes!" he shouted, running across the room and snatching the paper out of Mr. Cowan's hand. *"Yes!"*

He hurried out of the room, only pausing in the doorway for a moment. "Thanks, Mr. Cowan," he said over his shoulder.

"Good luck in the game," the teacher called after him.

In the dressing room, Gavin quickly changed into his boots and Tigers uniform. Outside on the pitch, he saw the Cedars Secondary Vipers warming up in their green jerseys and black shorts. They were big. Really big.

Down at the far end of the pitch, Mido was leading the Tigers through a warm-up. The whole team was involved except for Blair, who was standing on the sidelines, juggling a soccer ball. The blond striker had a sour expression on his face.

Gavin jogged over to him. "Hey, what's up? Why aren't you warming up with the team?"

Blair spat sideways into the grass, then pointed at Mido. "He benched me last game."

Gavin saw Mido walking over. His friend had clearly overheard.

"Yeah, that's right, I benched you," he said fiercely. "And we were a better team."

"Big achievement," said Blair, rolling his eyes. "That other team sucked."

"Whatever, we still won, didn't we?" Mido snapped.

Blair took a step toward Mido, then gestured at Gavin. "I thought you were the coach, Gavin. But you're letting this little freak run the team. He's just jealous 'cause I'm a better player than him."

Blair's right, thought Gavin. *He is a better player than Mido.* But everything the blond-haired striker had just said was about himself. None of it was about the team. Gavin remembered Dizzy Deano. The gaffer had benched the player to send him a message. Blair hadn't got the message yet.

"Mido's right," Gavin told Blair. "You're benched."

"I knew you'd do whatever Mido said," hissed the blond-haired striker. "You're a fake. You're no coach."

It was then that Gavin noticed one of the Tiny Giants standing on the sidelines with crutches under his armpits.

"What are we going to do about that?" he asked Mido.

"Simple. Same as last game," said Mido slowly. "Derek in defence for Mikey. Lucas up front with you, instead of Blair."

"Mikey?" said Gavin, puzzled. "Lucas?"

"Him and him," said Mido, pointing at the injured Tiny Giant, then at Jeans Guy.

Oh no, thought Gavin. He glanced over at Blair.

The teams entered the field and prepared for kick-off. Gavin scanned the sidelines. He remembered how many fans had been at the St. Michael's game. Here, there were only a few parents.

But the one fan Gavin cared about most, the one with a big coat and an old peaked cap, was nowhere to be seen.

The referee blew one long blast on his whistle. A Cedars player kicked the ball to his teammate, who took a long shot on Critter. Critter caught it easily.

"Hey," said someone to Gavin's right.

Gavin looked. It was Jeans Guy. *Lucas*, Gavin told himself. "What do you want?" he said quickly.

"I've never played striker," said Lucas. "I don't know what to do."

But just then, Critter's long drop kick sailed toward skinny Jamie. He jumped higher than the huge Cedars midfielders and headed the ball toward Gavin. Gavin flicked it over a defender's lunging boot, then passed the ball out to the side for Lucas.

The ball thudded off the awkward boy's shin pad and rolled way wide of the goal.

"Good try, Lucas!" shouted Mido.

It was then that Gavin knew what he needed to do. "Just chase the defenders when they get the ball," he told Lucas. "And if you get the chance to shoot, don't look at your target. Just concentrate on kicking the ball!"

A Cedars defender gathered the ball and tried to dribble down the line. Lucas charged over and tackled him, awkwardly but cleanly.

Now that's coaching! thought Gavin.

Lucas tried to pass the ball into the centre. But he flubbed his kick, and the ball rolled out again.

Or not, Gavin reconsidered, glancing at Blair again.

"Keep going, Lucas!" shouted Mido.

Maybe I need to be a bit more patient, thought Gavin.

The goal kick soared over his head. He turned and watched as a big Vipers midfielder headed the ball toward the Tigers defence.

Derek tried to jump to head it away from danger. But as he jumped, the ball skimmed off the back of his head. A speedy little Vipers striker zipped in and smashed a shot into the top corner of the Vandyke goal. He pumped his fist in the air.

"That's okay, Derek!" said Mido, giving the defender a pat on the back. "Good try. We'll get it back."

It's good to be positive, thought Gavin. *But it's not going to win us this game.*

From the restart, Lucas lost the ball again. But he chased the player and tackled him hard, winning the ball back.

"Over here!" shouted Gavin. He heard Jamie shouting behind him, too.

Once again, Lucas flubbed his kick, giving away the ball to the Vipers, who surged forward in a counterattack.

Mido managed to tackle their striker. The ball bounced away. Derek swung his leg but missed and kicked nothing but air.

The speedy Cedars striker scrambled up. Steadying himself, he lashed a shot that sizzled toward Critter's top left corner.

Critter launched himself upward like a rocket. Somehow he tipped the ball up and over the crossbar.

The referee whistled for halftime.

As the teams jogged off the field, Gavin glanced at the spectators. *Still no sign of Granddad.* Coach Sonderhoff was there, sitting in the back bleachers, reading a book.

Gavin looked around at his teammates. They were all looking down at the ground, shoulders slumped.

Look at us, thought Gavin. *It's like we've already lost.*

Critter walked over. "Gavin," he said quietly.

"Yeah?"

"You need to do something."

"What do you mean?"

"You need to get this team going," said Critter. "Come on — you're the coach!"

Gavin looked away. "Am I? I mean, seems like things went better last game when Mido was in charge. Maybe he's a better coach."

"No offence to Mido's coaching skills," said Critter, looked at Gavin, "but my little brother's team could have won that game. And yeah, Mido's always positive, a great team player and all, but you started this team, and the guys all know you're the one who's coach. You're their leader on the field. Now, you need to be their leader off the field too."

He doesn't get it, thought Gavin. *Everything I do goes wrong.*

"Gav, if you don't do something, no one will. We'll lose this game. Don't you want another chance at St. Mike's?"

Gavin closed his eyes. "Guys, follow me!" he called out.

He walked to a part of the field away from the spectators. "You too," he said to Blair. "And you." He pointed to Mikey, the Tiny Giant on crutches.

Gavin looked at the circle of orange shirts. All eyes

were focused on him. He knew Critter was right: He had to say something. But what the heck was he supposed to say?

"Guys," he said, his voice cracking. "We're still in this game, you know, but we need to, sort of —"

"— keep going, guys!" Mido interrupted. "We're doing well, no worries at all, just need to —"

Something inside Gavin snapped. "Mido, shut up!"

He regretted the words immediately. *Mido's my best friend*, his heart told him. But there was no going back. He'd said it.

"Look," he said shakily, "we're not doing badly. We're only down one. But we need to concentrate on making solid contact with the ball. There've been too many bad kicks and sloppy passes." He glanced at Lucas and Derek. Everyone noticed. *Damn it*, thought Gavin.

But something told him to keep going. "You two especially," he said to them. "You're working hard, but you need to get your body behind the ball every time you can. Someone give me a ball."

Critter rolled one to him.

Gavin demonstrated. "See? Like this."

He looked up. Lucas and Derek were both nodding.

Blair stepped forward. "Bravo, Coach. You finally stopped listening to Short Stuff here." He pointed at Mido. "So why don't you put me in? If I'm in, we win. Simple."

"No," said Gavin. "You just want to show off. You don't come back and defend. You're not a team player. So, no."

Blair stormed away.

Out on the field, the referee blew his whistle.

"Good job, Coach G," said Critter as they ran out for the second half. Gavin saw Mido standing in his usual defensive position. He seemed to be avoiding Gavin's eyes.

The second half kicked off. Right away, the Vipers attacked. Their quick little striker stepped around Derek as if he were a big orange cone, then curled a shot toward Critter's net.

The lanky goalkeeper dove sideways and wrestled the ball to the ground.

His kick cleared Gavin and bounced on to the foot of a Cedars defender. Lucas tackled the ball away and tried to pass to Gavin. Once again, he mis-kicked. The ball rolled out for a throw-in.

At last, Gavin knew what to do.

"Jeans G— I mean, Lucas," he called out. "Switch with Derek."

Lucas looked confused for a moment, but then nodded. He jogged back and sent Derek forward.

"Just use your size and strength to get to long high balls first," said Gavin when the redhead had rumbled forward. "Head them, knee them, kick them, bounce them off your belly — just get to them first."

"Got it," said Derek, his face red and shirt soaked with sweat.

Jamie intercepted the Vipers throw-in and chipped the ball forward.

Derek jumped. Or tried to jump. The ball bounced off the top of his head.

Gavin surged forward, straining every muscle. He brushed past the last defender, stealing the ball away. His shot sizzled along the ground into the bottom left corner of the net. The goalkeeper stood there stunned, feet rooted to the ground.

Gavin sprinted into the net to get the ball, ignoring his cheering teammates. There was no time to celebrate. The game was tied 1–1. Only a win would get them to the city final.

After the kickoff the speedy little striker tried once more to dribble through the Tigers' defence. Lucas sent him sprawling this time with a clean tackle. One of the Tiny Giants cleared the ball.

A defender jumped next to Derek, but looked down at the hefty Tigers player and lost his concentration. The ball spun away wildly off Derek's knee.

Gavin reached it just before the Cedars goalkeeper.

"Over here!" someone shouted to his left.

Gavin slipped the ball sideways. The goalkeeper's arm clattered against his shin pads.

As he tumbled to the ground, he saw Jamie scoop the ball wide of the empty goal with his left foot.

So close!

"Good pass," said Jamie as they ran back. "I should have scored."

"Forget it," said Gavin. "Focus on the next one."

The speedy Cedars striker refused to give up. He stepped past a Tiny Giant, then swerved around Mido's desperate lunge. Lucas chased after him. Critter charged off his line.

The shot was flying toward Critter, but then ricocheted off Lucas's toe away from the keeper. The ball dribbled toward the goal line. Closer, closer, closer . . .

No! Gavin clenched his teeth. *Not after coming back from 1–0 down.*

Just as the ball was about to cross the line, Lucas slid in and kicked it away,

Gavin nearly collapsed in relief. But then he realized the ball was still in play. Jamie had it and was racing down the left side.

"Jamie!" he shouted, sprinting into the middle.

The pass sliced right through the heart of the Vipers defence. Gavin pushed the ball forward. Too far forward. The keeper charged, blocking off the angle.

But there was help to Gavin's right. "Over here!" called a voice.

Later, Gavin had to admit that if he'd known it was Derek, he wouldn't have passed. But he didn't know, so he slipped the ball sideways, just before the goalkeeper knocked him flying again.

The ball sliced wildly off Derek's right boot. It rebounded off the post, rolling right along the goal line.

Gavin leaped to his feet. Derek was racing two Cedars defenders. The chubby player seemed destined to lose the race. But at the last moment, he hurled his whole body forward. The ball flew off his big belly into the back of the net.

Gavin tried to jump on Derek, but bounced off and tumbled to the ground. Soon the whole Tigers team was mobbing them both, cheering and whooping.

Minutes later the final whistle sounded. The whole team charged toward Derek again. He tried to run away, but they caught him easily and pulled him to the ground.

"Great game, Coach," said someone, clapping Gavin on the shoulder.

Gavin turned to see who it was, but he couldn't tell with everyone crowded around.

In the distance, he could see Coach Sonderhoff on his feet. The big man was applauding. He caught Gavin's eye and pumped a fist in the air.

But next to the bleachers stood a small solitary figure in an orange shirt, soccer bag slung over a shoulder. As the Vandyke Tigers celebrated all around him, Gavin watched Mido take one more look at the pitch, then turn and walk away.

Gavin started toward him. Things had gone far enough. He needed to go after his friend.

But before he could get to Mido, Gavin saw some-one running toward him. It was his father, red-faced, breathing hard.

"Gavin," he said. "We need go to the hospital. It's Granddad."

13 GRANDDAD

"He had a fall, Gav," said Gavin's father when they got to the car. "He tripped going down the back steps."

Gavin let out a sigh of relief. A fall was just a fall. Wasn't it?

When they reached the hospital, Gavin followed his father into the big, grey building.

It wasn't like Gavin hadn't been to the hospital before. There was the time he'd sprained his ankle, back in Grade Six. And once, when he was little, he'd needed seven stitches in his knee after falling off his bike.

But this time, walking through the long white-walled corridors with his father, something felt different. It was as if there was something important about this moment, something he needed to remember.

He tried to shrug off the strangeness of the feeling. *Stop being silly*, he told himself.

Gavin's father stopped and pointed to an open door. "He's in there," he said in a low voice.

As Gavin entered the room, he saw his mother

perched on a seat next to a bed. She rose to her feet.

"Gav," she said, walking across the room and wrapping her arms around him.

At that moment, Gavin knew Granddad's fall wasn't just a fall. It was something far more serious.

He pressed his lips together tightly.

"Hello, mate," said a crackly old voice.

Gavin pulled away from his mother. He saw a familiar face staring back at him from the hospital bed. Only it wasn't familiar. The skin was so pale it seemed almost transparent. The cheeks sagged. And the eyes seemed to be staring off into the distance.

But as those same eyes settled on Gavin, a smile spread across that old wrinkled face, and it became familiar again.

Granddad beckoned weakly. "Why don't you come sit down? We can't have everyone standing around like statues, can we?"

Gavin took two steps forward.

His mother put a hand in front of him. "Dad, are you sure you're not too tired?"

Granddad waved her away. "Never too tired to speak to my grandson."

She turned and left the room. Gavin saw tears in her eyes. He sat down in the chair next to the bed and looked at his grandfather.

"Had a bit of a tumble, eh, Granddad?"

Granddad nodded. "Oh yes. Not to worry. Right as

rain before you know it."

Gavin sat still, listening to the quiet beep of the hospital machines. Behind the curtain next to the bed, someone was snoring loudly.

"That old git never stops sawing wood," whispered Granddad. "So anyway, Gav, about that game today . . ."

Gavin felt a surge of guilt. While he'd been off playing soccer, something terrible had happened to Granddad.

"It's okay," he said. "We don't need to talk about soccer. It's not important."

Granddad pushed himself up against the pillows behind him. He looked at Gavin. A little colour flowed back into his cheeks. There was fire in his eyes. "Not important?" he exclaimed. "What are you talking about? Come on, m'boy, out with it. What happened?"

Gavin told Granddad everything. About the difficult first half. About Critter's saves. About switching Lucas and Derek, and the second half comeback. He even talked about his halftime speech and what had happened with Blair. And Mido.

"He's really mad at me," said Gavin. "I don't know what to do."

Granddad nodded solemnly. "I'm proud of you, mate."

Gavin felt tears heating up behind his eyes. He had never heard his grandfather say those words before.

"You took risks," said Granddad, reaching for his

cup of water. "In the end, taking risks pays off. Not always right away, but in the end, it does. I remember one game when the old gaffer . . ."

He trailed off. "Forget it. I'm sorry I always tell you these boring old stories."

Gavin wanted to tell Granddad that his stories weren't boring. They were the best stories in the whole world. He would never ever get tired of them. But somehow he couldn't force the words out through his lips.

"You remember when I first moved to Canada?" asked Granddad.

Gavin nodded. He'd been seven at the time, but he could play those days through his mind like a movie.

"I've never told anyone this before, but moving to Canada was one of the biggest risks of my life," said Granddad softly. "Your grandmother and I, we met when we were teenagers. We were always together. And so, when she passed away, I didn't know what to do. I'd never felt so alone. I was like one of those people in storybooks, trapped on an empty island.

"Your mother," he continued. "She was worried about me. She suggested I move to Canada. Well, I'd visited Canada a few times, and I liked it. So I thought I'd give it a go."

He paused to cough. Gavin passed him another cup of water.

"When I moved here, I missed England so much," Granddad went on. "But then I saw you play football in a match for the first time. That was when I knew I would stay. You and your football. You helped me escape that empty lonely island."

A tear ran down Granddad's cheek. Gavin handed him a tissue from the box next to the bed.

"Thank you, m'boy." His grandfather wiped his eyes, then blew his nose like a trumpet. "Look at me — silly old man, blubbering like a fool."

Gavin saw his mother come back into the room. "I think we need to give Granddad a chance to sleep," she said calmly.

The old man nodded. "I think your mother's right, Gavin. Need to rest up so I'm fit for your big match!"

"You sound like you're going to play, Granddad," said Gavin, laughing despite the heaviness in his chest.

"If I could lace up my boots, I'd be the first one on the pitch," said the old man.

"By the way," he added, leaning toward Gavin, "next time you see Mido, maybe find a way to show that you appreciate what he brings to the team."

"All right, you two," said Gavin's mother. "Time to say good night."

Gavin made it halfway across the room before he decided to turn back. Walking back to the bed, he put one arm around his grandfather. Then he squeezed one of the old man's hands in his own.

"Good night, Granddad," he said.

His mother was standing in the doorway. As Gavin

approached, she stepped into the hallway.

A nurse stepped past them into Granddad's room. She flicked a light switch and the room went dark.

"What did you two talk about?" asked Gavin's mother as they walked away together.

Gavin thought about everything his grandfather had said. "He told me he was proud of me." It was all he could get out.

Gavin's mother put an arm around his shoulder. "So are we, buddy," she said. "So are we."

★★★

Gavin put his bag down on the change room floor. He turned to Critter. "So, is he coming or not?"

The goalkeeper shrugged. "I don't know. He's been avoiding me too."

Mr. Cowan had been so amazed Gavin and Critter had finished all their work that he let them both out of their math class ten minutes early.

"Go win that final," he'd told them.

Gavin had felt a little guilty. He'd let Critter copy his answers.

Players started coming into the room, laughing and chatting nervously. Jamie, Lucas, Derek, Blair, the four Tiny Giants . . .

But no Mido.

Gavin had tried phoning his friend. He'd tried

emailing him. He'd tried talking to him in person, but Mido had just muttered something under his breath and walked away.

As Gavin laced up his boots, he thought about what Granddad had said. That taking chances usually paid off.

Sure, Gavin thought, *it pays off in soccer. But is it worth losing one of my best friends?*

He'd been to visit Granddad every day that week. The old man's condition had improved a little. Now he spent some time sitting upright, watching television or reading the newspapers Gavin brought from home. But Gavin knew there was no way Granddad would be well enough to come to the city final.

Critter had even come along to the hospital once.

"You're much better than any goalkeeper we ever had back in Ipswich," Granddad had told him. "We spent most of our time on defence trying to make sure our keepers never had to touch the ball!"

Gavin finished tying up his left boot. He smiled. *That sure put a big goofy grin on Critter's face.*

"Gav. It's time to get out there."

Gavin looked up. Critter was standing in front of him, gloves and boots on, ready to go.

Gavin stood up. The rest of the players stood up too. Nerves swirled in Gavin's stomach. Could they really beat St. Mike's? Did they even stand a chance?

"Guys, wait!"

Gavin spun around.

Mido was struggling into the room with a big black duffel bag. He dropped it in the middle of the room and wrenched the zipper open. "Look! Proper uniforms!"

Gavin stood there, stunned. "Mido, how did you —"

"Never mind," said Mido, tossing out shorts and shirts. "I'll explain later."

Gavin caught a uniform, then froze. Every player in the room was looking at him. He paused, but then pulled off his old shirt and tugged on a new one. "Hurry up, guys. What are you waiting for?"

All around, there was a flurry of orange and black as players switched into their sleek new uniforms.

Gavin turned to Mido and said quietly, "These are amazing. How'd you do it?"

"My dad's company," said Mido. "I've been working on him since the first practice to sponsor our team."

Gavin thought for a moment. "Meeds, I'm sorry about last game. You did so well coaching the Templeton game and I wasn't sure what to do. I thought you wanted to be coach. But this — this is amazing."

"You're the coach," replied Mido. "I'm just here to help."

14 TAKING ONE FOR THE TEAM

"What in the world?" Gavin blinked as he led his team down to the field.

More than a hundred students were standing or sitting next to the main Vandyke football field, now converted to a soccer pitch with goals and markings. Most of the students were decked out in orange and black. A few were holding signs that said GO TIGERS or COME ON, VANDYKE!

"Cheerleaders!" gasped one of the Tiny Giants.

Gavin turned to Critter. "How did this happen?"

"You remember when I talked to Coach Sonderhoff?" replied Critter. "We made a deal. He said he'd let us use the main field and get a crowd out and I said I'd —"

"Let's go, Tigers!" A group of huge football players had suddenly surrounded Gavin, Critter, and the rest of the soccer team. They were all wearing their Vandyke Tigers jerseys, and were cheering and pumping their fists.

Gavin felt someone give him a thump on the back.

"Go get 'em, Coach G!"

Out in the middle of the pitch, the referee blew his whistle.

As coach and captain, Gavin jogged to the centre. Craig was waiting next to the referee, an arrogant sneer on his face.

"Nice turnout," he said mockingly. "I'm going to enjoy embarrassing you in front of your friends."

Gavin ignored him.

The referee tossed a quarter into the air and caught it on the back of his hand.

"First ball, Tigers," he announced.

There was a huge roar from the Vandyke supporters. Gavin was surprised. He'd never heard anyone cheer the coin toss before.

"That's the only thing you'll win today," hissed Craig.

As the teams lined up, Gavin looked over at the St. Mike's coach. He was next to the field, shouting last-minute instructions at his team. Just down the sidelines stood the injured Tiny Giant, on crutches, and Blair.

And all around them, the cheering Vandyke crowd.

Forget the crowd, Gavin told himself. He stared down at the ball. *Forget Craig. Forget Blair.*

Tweeeeee!

He tapped the ball to Derek, then sprinted away. The return pass came quickly. Gavin controlled the ball easily, then slipped it through a charging defender's legs.

Thwack! A boot hit Gavin's shin pad, knocking him to the turf.

Gavin rolled over onto his side, grabbing his left shin. His leg was on fire.

Mido ran over and shoved Craig. "What the hell, man!"

"Mido!" Gavin shouted, returning painfully to his feet. "Let it go. I'm okay."

The referee beckoned Craig and Mido.

Yellow card. Yellow card.

Mido took the free kick, sending it high into the St. Mike's area. Gavin saw Derek move to head the ball and rushed behind his big teammate, ignoring the pain in his leg.

The ball bounced off Derek's head, landing right in front of Gavin. He spun around. No defenders. He was all alone, with only the keeper to beat. He could hardly believe his luck.

People were shouting from every direction.

"Shoot!"

"Score!"

"Do it, Gavin!"

As he swung his leg at the ball, Gavin thought he heard a faint whistling sound. With all the noise from the crowd, he wasn't sure. So as the ball curled into the far corner of the net, Gavin turned and looked over at the far side of the field. The referee's assistant had raised his flag.

"No goal," shouted the referee, jogging toward Gavin. "It's offside."

"Ref, he shot the ball after the whistle," whined the St. Mike's keeper.

"Number seven, come here," said the referee.

Gavin pointed at himself. "Me?"

"Come here," the referee repeated, pointing to the ground in front of him.

Gavin jogged over. The referee reached into his pocket. Yellow card.

"What's that for?" exclaimed Gavin. All around, Tigers supporters complained loudly from the sidelines.

"Kicking the ball after the whistle."

I barely heard the whistle, Gavin wanted to scream. *And I'd already kicked the ball!* He forced himself to stay silent. If he got a red card, he would let the whole team down.

The Stallions goalkeeper put the ball on the ground, then thumped it forward.

Farther up the pitch, the Stallions big skinhead striker outjumped everyone. His header bounced toward Lucas.

Lucas swung his foot and missed the ball. The Stallions striker nicked it away and raced down the right side of the pitch. He sent a cross into the middle. Gavin held his breath. It looked dangerous. But Critter raced off his line and leaped above Craig, catching it easily. Before the tall keeper kicked the ball, he gave

Lucas a quick pat on the back.

Gavin got to Critter's long kick before anyone else. Two defenders blocked his way to the goal. He danced past one, then the other.

The keeper charged. To his right Gavin spotted Derek, barrelling toward the goal. Remembering the Cedars game, he slipped the ball sideways.

The big guy's foot connected solidly with the ball. Gavin watched as it soared up, up . . .

. . . and just over the crossbar.

Groans all around the field.

Gavin nearly collapsed. *Defenders gone. Keeper down. Empty goal.*

Derek stared at the goal, his hands on his head clutching clumps of his curly red hair.

Gavin walked over to him.

"Unlucky, man," he said, putting a hand on the Derek's shoulder. "Come on. Let's get the next one!"

As Gavin ran back, he heard the St. Michael's goal-keeper screaming at his defenders.

"Shut up and do your own job," shouted one of the defenders.

Like a pack of animals, thought Gavin. *They're turning against each other.*

With halftime approaching, the Stallions striker tried a shot. One of the Tiny Giants slid to block. The ball ricocheted off his leg and flew wide of the net. Corner kick.

"Gav, get back and defend," shouted Mido. "One minute till halftime!"

I'm the striker, thought Gavin. But then he remembered Blair's attitude and decided to run back to help out.

The ball sailed across the front of the goal. Gavin leaped as high as he could. It wasn't enough. He heard a head thump the ball behind him.

He turned in time to see Craig shove Mido out of the way to get to the ball. Critter charged to block the shot. Panicking at the sight of the Tigers keeper, Craig kicked wildly at the ball. His shot dribbled harmlessly wide of the net. But he flew into the air dramatically and fell to the ground, clutching his ankle.

Tweeee! The referee pointed to the penalty spot.

Critter stood, holding his hands up in disbelief. "I didn't touch him!" he hollered. "That was a dive!"

The referee walked over and gave Critter a yellow card. *Three friends, three yellow cards*, thought Gavin. *We'd better watch out.*

"Come on, Critter," he said, walking over and whacking his friend on the back. "You can save this."

Behind them, Craig and the bald striker were arguing about who was going to take the penalty kick. As Gavin took up his position, Craig pushed the striker out of the way, then put the ball on the penalty spot.

"Come on, Critter," Gavin hollered. *Anyone but Craig.*

The shot was a good one, low, to Critter's right. The tall keeper flung himself across the goal. The ball smacked against his right arm. *What a save!*

But before the Tigers could get to the rebound, Craig scuffed the ball into the net. It was 1–0 St. Michael's.

The whistle blew for halftime.

Gavin and his Vandyke teammates ran off the field to defiant cheers.

"Come on, Tigers! It's not over yet!"

"Hang in there, guys!"

"Only 1–0!"

The team gathered around Gavin at the edge of the field.

"I didn't even touch him!" Critter complained loudly.

"That was such a *dive*," whined one of the Tiny Giants.

Everyone joined at once, complaining about the referee, Craig, the skinhead striker.

"Gavin," said Mido quietly, "I know you're the coach. But do you mind if I say something?"

Gavin looked at his friend and nodded. "Go for it. Guys, listen up!"

Everyone stopped talking.

Mido pointed to the St. Mike's bench. The Stallions coach was red in the face, shouting at the players. None of them seemed to be listening. They were too busy arguing with one another.

Mido cleared his throat. "We're a way better *team* than St. Mike's," he said. "They got one lucky break. Yes, I know it was a bad call. But if we let ourselves fall apart over that, we've already lost."

Everyone looked at Gavin.

"Mido's right," he said. "Look at those guys — fighting over who takes the penalty shot, arguing about whose fault everything is . . ."

Critter spoke up. "Let's keep it together, eh? Play as a team. It's the only way we can come back and win."

The players cheered.

As they walked out onto the field for the second half, Gavin felt someone tap him on the shoulder.

It was Blair.

"Hey," he said, looking down at the ground. "I want in. I mean, I want to help the team. I want us to win."

His skills might help us out there, thought Gavin. *But can I trust him?*

"I'll think about it," he told the blond striker. "If we need a sub later, maybe."

Blair nodded. "That's okay. I can take one for the team."

Cheers from the crowd followed the Vandyke players out onto the field.

"Come on, guys!" shouted Lucas.

"Let's give this crowd something to cheer about!" said Gavin. His right shin was throbbing. The pain was getting harder to ignore.

From the kickoff, the ball went wide to a Stallions midfielder. The player passed to the skinhead striker. The striker looked up. He clearly saw Craig, but tried to dribble instead of passing.

Lucas tackled hard, stealing the ball. The striker tumbled to the ground. Lucas looped the ball away. Mido controlled it on his chest, then sent a hard pass toward Gavin.

Taking the ball in his stride, Gavin muscled around the Stallions central defender. Another defender cut across to challenge the ball, but stumbled.

"Gav!"

Derek again. Gavin remembered the empty goal in the first half.

Win as a team, lose as a team, he thought. He passed the ball.

Derek took a shot, but scuffed it so badly it bounced back to Gavin.

The goalkeeper had shuffled across the goal toward Derek and was out of position. Gavin smashed the ball into the open corner of the net.

"Great goal!"

High-fives, hugs and loud shouts were all around him. And all around the field, Tigers fans cheered their team.

When the action started again, Gavin lunged to stop Craig as he dribbled forward. Craig stomped down hard. Gavin fell to the ground, clutching his ankle.

Taking One for the Team

When he got up, he found he could barely walk.

Gavin bit his lip. *I've got to stay on*, he told himself. *It's the biggest game of the year.* He took another step. His ankle screamed with pain.

Gavin looked over at Blair on the sidelines. *It's my turn to take one for the team*, he decided.

The Tigers fans gasped as Gavin limped off. "I can't run," he said to Blair. "You ready?"

Blair ripped off his jacket and handed it to Gavin. After a quick high-five, he sprinted out onto the field.

Gavin glanced up at the big school clock. *Not much time left.*

A long ball flew into the Vandyke area, which Critter snagged. He hurled the ball forward. Just as Blair got to the ball, Gavin spotted the St. Mike's keeper. He was fifteen metres off his goal line.

"Blair!" shouted Gavin. "Shoot! Keeper's out!"

Blair sliced his foot under the ball. It rose and rose — then dropped and dropped. The keeper scrambled back frantically. At the last moment he threw himself up into the air. The ball skipped off his fingertips and flew just over the crossbar.

Gavin nearly collapsed in disappointment. *This is awful*, he thought, *standing on the sidelines.* His stomach was in knots. *I don't know how professional coaches do this every week.*

He looked up at the clock again. *Penalty shootout if we don't score now*, he thought. And there was still enough time for the Stallions to score on the counterattack.

"Guys," he called to his defenders. "Stay ba—"

Suddenly, he remembered what his grandfather had said about risks.

"Everyone up there!" he hollered. "Everyone. The whole team! You too, Critter."

The Tigers keeper pointed to himself. "Me?"

"Get up there!" shouted Gavin.

Critter ran forward, all lanky arms and legs.

"Nice strategy," scoffed the St. Michael's coach from farther down the sideline. "It's 1–1. Don't you know anything?"

Gavin ignored him.

Mido took the corner. It came in low and hard, clearing the jump of the Stallions keeper. Blair leaped. He headed the ball back across the goal.

Everyone seemed to jump for it at once. But out of the mess of orange-and-black shirts, Gavin saw one player rise above the rest.

The ball smashed against Critter's head and flew into the top left corner of the Stallions goal.

Gavin watched his big friend running straight for him, arms and legs spiralling like mad, teammates chasing after him.

Gavin was in shock. He couldn't move. It was a moment he'd never forget.

15 A WIN AND A LOSS

The waiting room was silent when Gavin and his parents arrived at the hospital the next day.

Gavin couldn't wait to talk to Granddad about the final. There was so much to tell.

"Go ahead," said the nurse at the desk. "The doctor's with him now."

As he walked into the room with his parents, Gavin heard the faint but steady sound of hospital machines.

Beep. Beep. Beep.

A man in a white coat was standing next to the bed. Gavin inhaled sharply when he saw his grandfather, paler than ever against the pillows. Granddad was struggling for breath.

Gavin started toward the bed. His father put a hand on his shoulder. "Just a moment, Gav."

The doctor walked toward them. He took off his glasses and sighed.

"I'm afraid the news is bad," he said. "Surgery last night and this morning failed to reverse the situation."

Gavin felt hot tears burn behind his eyes. He bit his lip. "Is he gonna . . . ?"

Granddad's weak voice came from the bed. "Gavin . . . you there? Come over here."

For Gavin, the short distance to the bed felt like one of the longest walks of his life. Granddad turned his head against the pillow slowly. His eyes were watery and only half-open. But as he looked at Gavin, he smiled weakly.

"Hello, mate," he whispered.

"Hello, Granddad." Gavin could hear the rasping sound of his grandfather's breathing.

"How'd you . . . get on last night?" the old man said.

"We won," said Gavin, "2–1."

The faint smile returned. "Smashing. Absolutely smashing."

The old man held out his hand. Gavin took it. The skin of Granddad's hand was cool to the touch. The grip was as weak as a little child's.

Looking down at the hand, Gavin wondered why his tears had gone away. "Granddad," he said, "I've got something to show you."

He pulled out a scrapbook from under his arm. It wasn't his Granddad's old brown scrapbook. It was a brand-new one with a bright orange cover.

Gavin opened it to the first page. There was a photo filled with grinning soccer players standing behind a big trophy.

"That's us, Granddad. City champions!"

Granddad peered at the photograph. "Nice . . . new uniforms."

"Mido got his dad's company to donate them," said Gavin.

He flipped through a few more photos, telling Granddad about the game. The near misses. The penalty. The hundreds of fans. His goal. His injury. Mido coming back to the team. The Critter miracle goal.

"Critter. . . scored a goal?" Granddad whispered.

Gavin nodded. "Hard to believe, but true."

Granddad turned his face toward the ceiling. "Reckon . . . I'd have liked . . . to have seen that."

For a time, Gavin sat there, grasping Granddad's hand, the two of them silent. Granddad closed his eyes. Gavin listened to him breathe.

"Gavin?"

Turning around, Gavin saw his mother standing at the foot of the bed.

"It's okay, Mom," he said. "It's okay."

★★★

The week after Granddad passed away, Gavin didn't go to school. The first day, he didn't even leave his room. He just lay on his bed, pretending to read soccer magazines. Mostly, he just stared out the window.

The soccer team had won the championship. Gavin

and Mido weren't fighting anymore. And Gavin had proven he could be a good coach — with a little help from his friends.

He thought about his grandmother. When Granddad had talked about her, Gavin hadn't really understood what the old man had meant about that feeling of being stranded on a lonely, empty island.

Now he understood. Because now, he was on that island.

He flung his magazine across the room. *Why do good things end? Why have them if they just leave us?*

On the morning of the third day he spent in his bedroom, Gavin's father came up to the bedroom before he left for work.

"Gav," he said, "maybe you should go to school today." He put a hand on his son's shoulder. "Your mother and I know what you're going through."

Part of Gavin wanted to scream back, *No, you don't! How could you? Get out of my room!* But he didn't.

"I just can't today," he said. He looked at his father. "I'll go on Monday, Dad. Promise."

He fell asleep early on Friday night, still wearing all his clothes. When he awoke, his dinner was sitting on the desk next to the window, cold and half-eaten.

Yawning, he picked up the plate and slumped out of the room. He started slowly down the stairs.

"Morning, honey."

Gavin's mother was standing near the bottom of

the stairs. Behind her, in the living room, was the entire Vandyke Tigers soccer team. Mido, Critter, Blair, the Tiny Giants — everyone.

Gavin's father poked his head into the room from the kitchen. He had a spatula in his hand. "Morning, Gav! Your whole *football* team's here."

Gavin stayed rooted to the spot at the bottom of the stairs. It was as if his feet were frozen to the carpet. He looked out at all the concerned friendly faces. He wasn't quite sure how to feel.

"Mom," he said, "why did you do this?"

"I didn't," she said simply, shrugging her shoulders. "Around seven-thirty, they all just kind of started showing up. And some brought bacon and eggs."

Critter and Mido walked over to Gavin. Critter put an arm around his shoulders. "Soccer Saturday forever, right, Coach G?"

"It's a good thing your dad was here," said Mido. "Critter was threatening to cook the bacon and eggs himself."

"A whole soccer team with the runs — that'd be fun," joked Blair from the floor in front of the couch.

Critter and Mido led Gavin to his grandfather's favourite old brown chair. Gavin hesitated, then sat. It felt strange to sit in the chair. Not unpleasant, just strange.

On television, a game was about to begin. Manchester City was playing, and so were Gavin's beloved Wolves.

"You know what?" said Gavin. "I never realized it before, but Wolves have got the same colour jerseys as us Tigers."

"Doesn't mean I'm ever going to support them," said Mido. "Liverpool all the way."

And then everyone started arguing about which teams and players were best.

Gavin's father walked in from the kitchen with a plate stacked high with eggs, bacon, and toast, along with a glass of orange juice. The living room was too crowded for his dad to enter, so the guys passed the plate along to Gavin.

"Want some?" Gavin said to the Tiny Giant next to him.

"I'm full," said the kid, pointing to his stomach. "Already had some."

Gavin's half-eaten dinner from the night before was now a distant memory. And so he ate every bit of the breakfast. It was delicious.

On the TV, Wolves scored with a beautiful curling shot right into the top left corner of the net.

"There you go, Gav," said Critter.

"They've still got lots of time to lose," said Mido.

Gavin looked around the room. He still couldn't believe it. Just a few weeks ago, the Vandyke Tigers had been a pack of animals. Now they were a team.

"Hey guys," he said. "What are things like at school — since the big game? Is everyone into soccer now?"

Derek shifted his bulk around to face Gavin. "You know Vandyke," he said. "Football, football, football."

"That's not true," said Critter. "Lots of people have been coming up and congratulating me this week. Even the football guys."

"That's because you're one of them," replied Lucas. There was a chorus of teasing, all directed at Critter.

"Wait . . . what?" said Gavin.

"He doesn't know, Critter," said Mido.

Critter looked at Gavin sheepishly. "I tried to tell you before the final. You remember how I said I made a deal with Coach Sonderhoff, so that he'd get the football guys and cheerleaders out to support us?"

Gavin nodded, still confused.

Critter continued. "Well, he said he'd only do it if I joined the football team as a wide receiver."

Gavin's jaw dropped. "You joined the football team?"

"Yeah," said Critter. "My first game's tonight. The whole team's coming."

Gavin didn't know what to say.

"You're welcome to come too, Gav," said Critter. "But if you don't, it's okay. I know you aren't the biggest fan of that kind of football."

"N-no," stammered Gavin. "I'll be there. Everyone's going?"

"You bet," said Mido. "Kickoff's at six-thirty. I can't wait to see Critter get rocked." Critter swung a lanky arm at him. Mido ducked.

Critter on the football team, thought Gavin. *What would Granddad say to that?*

While he'd been talking with the guys, the heavy feeling in his chest had lifted for the first time since he'd lost Granddad. Now it was back. He was on that cold, lonely island again. He was alone.

But then he remembered what Granddad had said about leaving England. That somehow, watching Gavin play soccer in Canada had helped him move on after losing someone he loved.

Gavin looked around the room at his friends, at the game on the television, at the tattered old scrapbook on the coffee table.

Soccer Saturdays would never be the same again. He would always miss Granddad, every single day. But at least he would remember the good times too. There had been so many good times. He'd gained so much by having Granddad in his life.

"Final score: 1–0," said Critter, turning toward Gavin. "Looks like your team has finally won."

ACKNOWLEDGEMENTS

I would like to thank some of the people who helped me with *Playing Favourites*. Editors Carrie Gleason, Kat Mototsune, and Maryan Gibson provided the kind of feedback that helps an author reinvent and reshape a rough scramble of ideas into a story. My agent, Monica Pacheco, was instructive and helpful during all stages of the publication process. Eparama Tuibenau designed a website to help promote the novel (http://trevorkew.com), which turned out to be more fun than I'd ever imagined. Over the years, my family has been incredibly supportive of my twin obsessions, soccer and writing (although I know my mother leans toward writing, as it doesn't cause quite so many injuries as the other one) — and this time was no different. My students and coworkers at Yokohama International School have been enthusiastic supporters as well, some even lending their first names or surnames to characters in my books. Lastly, Misako Takahashi — this book was the most enjoyable of all, because you were there beside me.

ありがとうございました。

MORE SPORTS, MORE ACTION
www.lorimer.ca

CHECK OUT THESE OTHER SOCCER STORIES FROM LORIMER'S SPORTS STORIES SERIES:

PLAYING FOR KEEPS
By Steven Sandor

Branko's small town lives and breathes hockey, which makes a star soccer keeper like him feel like an outsider. It's not until a video of a spectacular save he makes goes viral that he discovers acceptance is a two-way street.

BREAKAWAY
By Trevor Kew

When Adam's new friend Rodrigo introduces him to soccer, it doesn't take long for Adam to figure out why it's called the beautiful game … but it'll take a whole lot more time to convince his dad to let him play.

TRADING GOALS
By Trevor Kew

Vicky lives for soccer and dreams of being on the national team. But when she suddenly has to switch schools, she finds herself on the same team as her fiercest rival, a goalkeeper named Britney — and there's only room for one keeper in net.

SIDELINED
By Trevor Kew

Vicky's select team is bound for a tournament in England — the chance of a lifetime! But when a rivalry with her teammate erupts and interest in the same guy drives Vicky and her teammate apart, Vicky learns that no team is invincible.

CORNER KICK
By Bill Swan

Michael Strike's the most popular guy in school and the most talented soccer player around. But then a new kid from Afghanistan arrives who can show him up on the field and threatens to steal the spotlight.

FALLING STAR
By Robert Rayner

He's super-talented on the pitch, but lately Edison seems to have lost his nerve. He hesitates and misses shot after shot. Can a ragtag group of soccer misfits show him what the game is really about before it's too late?

JUST FOR KICKS
By Robert Rayner

Toby's not the greatest or most athletic player on the field, but he sure loves to play. That is until his new coaches try to reorganize his neighbourhood's pickup soccer games into a league. It suddenly no longer matters who's friend, foe, or family — it only matters who wins.

LITTLE'S LOSERS
By Robert Rayner

The Brunswick Valley soccer team isn't just bad — they're terrible. The worst. So awful, in fact, that their coach up and quits. No one is more surprised than they are to find out they've made it to the playoffs ... but who will coach them now?

SUSPENDED
By Robert Rayner

There's a new principal at Brunswick Valley School and the establishment is out to shut down the soccer team. For team captain Shay Sutton, the only way to fight fire is with fire, so he enlists the aid of two high school thugs to help the team.

DATE DUE
